TO BE, MAYBE

YAZHINI CHANDROO

Made with ♥ on the Notion Press Platform
www.notionpress.com

*For the ones who are still figuring out their stillness in silence—
and the ones who chose to sit beside them, quietly*

Contents

Acknowledgements   *vii*

1. Present   1

2. Past   7

3. Present   12

4. Past   16

5. Present   20

6. Past   25

7. Present   28

8. Past   32

9. Present   35

10. Past   39

11. Present   43

12. Past   47

13. Present   51

14. Past   55

15. Present   61

16. Past   66

17. Present   71

18. Past   75

19. Present   79

20. Past   82

21. Present   87

22. Past   92

23. Present   96

Contents

24. Past   100

25. Present   105

26. Past   110

27. Present   114

28. Past   118

29. Present   122

30. Present   127

Acknowledgements

Between *Poised* and *To Be, Maybe*, there was a three-year writing gap. I put this draft on pause more times than I can count, unsure whether it was a story I even wanted to share. But here it is—finally—and it wouldn't exist without a few people I'm endlessly grateful for.

To the readers who took *Poised* on their vacations, giving it the life I exactly dreamed of for it—thank you. You made me feel like maybe I was doing something right. You gave me hope to keep going.

To my mom and sister, for their unwavering support—this couldn't have happened without your patience.

To Tharak, who once told me that the antidote to a happy life is constantly exploring what makes your inner child happy. For me, it always came back to writing. You say profound things like it's nothing. Please don't ever change.

To Geer, who despite living miles away, is always a text away. Your updates and messages kept me sane through this process.

To Raksh, who has seen me through it all—and shown me there's something even greater than love: friendship.

To Ari, who's always down to talk about anything, at any time. My mind isn't a cluttered mess, thanks to you.

To Be, Maybe is a sad love letter to girlhood, to friendships, and—worst of all—to that feeling of staying stagnant while the world keeps moving. I was nineteen when I started this book, hoping I'd never have to publish it. It's messy. It's just feelings and fragments—no real plot. Who would want to read that? I thought, no one.

But you did.

And this one's for the people who really *get* it.

Because we've all been nineteen and stagnant at one point.

CHAPTER I

Present

The sound of waves crashing was the only companion to the brightly lit moon, water barely visible to Vienna as she adjusted her blue nightgown's strap whilst grabbing onto her scotch glass. She never was one to feel lonely when drinking, it made her particularly happy even, but on the piece of land where every path would lead to water that could drown out any type of feelings, it wasn't enough for her to drown out her loneliness on that particular night.

The scotch tasted exceptionally bitter to her, more than usual, she stared at the moon while she swallowed each sip, the view from her bed looked like something out of a movie, but she couldn't enjoy it. She couldn't even say why, she wished she could snatch the feeling right from her heart and throw it into the water that was not so far away from her, the wooden carved railing at the balcony that was about ten feet away from her bed.

She stood up and walked towards it, the water was somewhat visible now. The cold breeze hit her olive skin, making her shiver slightly. The satin hugging her body wasn't enough, but the goosebumps that came along with it made her feel oddly at ease. She put her hands on the railing and wished to look for the waves crashing but it was too dark, she hoped that the moonlight would help but it did its best it could. She touched the carvings, some kind of flower she really couldn't point out, she was too tired to be amused but she followed it, the vines that run through from the carved flowers gave her a sense of comfort, she wondered if jumping from the railing would make her happy. The waves carrying her away under the moonlight in an island where she barely knew anyone, even the sand below the railing would only be introduced to her if she ever decides to fall right then but she wouldn't let them to familiarize with her in a way that has to carry her ever so gracefully to her death.

Even to her, that sounded pathetic. She sighed and walked back to her bed; she wanted to block out the thoughts she wouldn't act upon.

On an island where everyone probably knew everyone, except the fleeting people like her who's there to attend her best friend's wedding, it sounded suffocating to be surrounded by water at all times.

The next morning when the sun was out and about, spilling from her huge windows onto her exposed skin, alongside the sound of the waves crashing, she could hear the sound of Carmel Synclare, she rubbed her right eye whilst she walked to her door to face her friend.

"It's 8 AM," Carmel barged in holding three bags which seemed like a lot for a pregnant woman to be holding. "We need coffee," she said as she sat on Vienna 's bed.

"No," Vienna said. "You need coffee, I just woke up, also, can pregnant women even have coffee?"

"Yes, I am allowed one cup of coffee per day," she said, "I also shopped."

"It's only 8 AM. Are the shops even open?" She didn't get the point of waking up any time before 10 AM but since she's out and about on a destination wedding for her best friend, she is always woken up by Carmy whose room is right next to hers, so whenever Carmy has a craving to shop or eat at ungodly hours, Vienna is there for her.

"Yes, the shops are open. This is a place where people come on vacations, you'd know that if you left your room."

You'd know that if you left your room," Carmy said as she lay down. "It's Petal's wedding, you can't just stay in your room."

Carmy thought Vienna was depressed, which was partly true. But Vienna was also just a homebody, and being one on vacation was a bummer to everyone around her.

"Why are we here for a wedding that's still three weeks away, I don't understand." But she did, Petal sat them both down and gave them a rundown, a month at the island - a week for lounging around, a week for partying, a week for preparing and rehearsals and the last week being the wedding week, Vienna wanted to be there for her friend and so she did. "You only want to hang out with me because Marcus couldn't come."

Carmy gasped, "that's not true, I'm glad he wasn't able to come, I haven't hung out with my girls in so long."

"See? That's another reason I don't get why," Vienna sat next to Carmy, "Petal's getting married and you're like 4 months pregnant and we're only twenty-four, we still have so much to see."

"You'll know when you meet your person, Vienna." Carmy sat up now and smiled, "Go get ready, we need to leave."

Vienna nodded, but she in fact will never get it even if she met her person. Meeting 'the one' was an urban legend created by old women to trick themselves into being happy with the men they ended up with. But deep down, Vienna knew—maybe even had a sliver of hope, when she looked at Carmy and her husband, or Petal and her fiancée.

Love existed all around her yet she felt too detached from it.

Vienna got ready to strut down the streets of people filled with bikinis and tan lines; She wore her sand-colored knitted dress while holding a cup of some green smoothie Carmy had gotten her. She pulled her sunglasses down from her hair and squinted against the sun. People at the nearby beach were playing volleyball—nothing of interest to her. In fact, being out wasn't in her best interest either, but she didn't want Carmy hanging out alone.

"You know, I don't really see myself doing anything here except go surfing and I don't know how to do that."

"Or you can look at guys who surf," Carmy winked at her and Vienna rolled her eyes, "Have some fun."

But fun for her ended as quickly as it could even start because as she squinted harder it seemed like she was looking at Eden Nightstone, her breathing became unsteady. She wasn't sure if it was actually him until Carmy gasped, "Is that Eden?

She didn't have to confirm, she knew. Of course she knew, she'd know him just from the strand of his hair. That blonde wavy hair – it was a mix of brunette and white really, his tanned skin and the height of someone that is distinct from everyone else.

Vienna could tell Eden apart from a million other men.

She stood up swiftly, "I'm leaving." But it was too late, she noticed that he was already walking towards them. She felt trapped, she had been preparing for this moment ever since she last saw him. Facing Eden again was on her bucket list and suddenly Carmy seemed right, she was on vacation, she is not curled up miserably in her room, she's halfway across the world for her best friend's wedding as her bridesmaid. That wasn't bad and not to mention she is a completely different person than when he last saw her.

He seemed to walk up casually like meeting her again wasn't big enough of a deal to him, like he wasn't looking forward to anticipating their next meeting. But as he came closer, she noticed that his face kind of looked sad, yet the same as ever. He hasn't changed a bit.

"Vienna?" he said with a questionable but an amusive look on his face. "No way it is you."

Vienna sat back down trying to hide her anxiousness, "It is me, flesh and bones."

He laughed, "wow," he said chuckling again. "This is crazy."

"I know right," she said. "Who would've thought we'd bump into each other, in this island, out of all places in the world." She too let out a laugh but for some reason it came out croaked.

"Well, it is apparently the place to be according to *Vogue Weddings*."

Carmy pitched in "Oh, that's why Petal wanted to get married here?"

Vienna just then noticed that Eden had a ball in his hand, he was fiddling with it like an anxious kid and just then she realized he is in fact was looking forward and anticipated meeting her as much as herself, but there was no signs of resentment on his face.

She wondered how he hasn't changed a bit at all in the last three years, she was glad she was wearing sunglasses so that no one can tell he was analyzing him.

"Wow," he said staring at Carmy "congrats." His eyebrows raised in his usual 'I'm happy' smile, his lips slightly turned upward but never fully, his eyebrows compensated for it.

Vienna nodded in agreement, not sure why she did that but she too realized, it was a habit that came out when she was with him. It was awkward suddenly, no one knew what to say. Whilst the sound of waves crashing in the middle of brightly lit sun, she suddenly did not find the sound comforting, she stared at Eden which a feeling in her chest that made her want to clutch it but before she could even react or do something to ease the tension, someone called his name out. He looked back and waved; she really didn't bother to make out who it was because she was glad for his distraction.

"Lovely meeting you guys," he said walking in reverse, almost movie-esque. "We'll catch up soon."

He stopped for a second. "I'm glad I ran into you again, Vivi."

As he ran back, she felt the warmth of long-lost familiarity at the unfamiliar place much better than the sound of waves that kept her company last night.

CHAPTER II

Past

About three years ago, Vienna met Eden at *Decords*. It was almost an exact copy of IKEA, except, for some reason, it was pricier - a secret haven that Vienna found out when she was on a house-hunt that failed drastically, instead she found her way into fake bedrooms.

She made it a routine to show up whenever she didn't want to be home—to almost feel like she could have it all. This time she was looking at ceramic soap trays shaped like clam shells, she didn't even use soaps, she used the huge bottle of vanilla scented body shampoo that Carmy gifted to her on her birthday but looking at those trays gave her a sense of comfort that maybe one day when she had her own house with bathroom big enough and more hours in a day which allowed her to think about what color of tray to use.

She walked slowly into the lamp aisle and wondered who uses lamps, what purpose do they serve exactly, what stopped them from turning on the big light but she thought about how her room's big lights are also the small lights so she was back at the ceramics, usually she found her way to the fake bedrooms that gave her a more welcoming feel than her own, but today she again wanted to look at the ceramic aisle because she has yet again found something that she could never afford to own and this time it was a grey plate that was shaped like a lavender, which is quite funny because they could have made it purple to make it look exactly like the flower yet it was grey and lifeless, she didn't know what that plate could be used for because it didn't seem like something people would eat off of but it looked cool and she wanted it. She turned the plate over and nodded whilst she looked for a price tag knowing she wouldn't be able to afford it anyway.

That's when she heard his voice.

"They could have made it purple," she turned around startled only to get more startled, he was taller, blonde hair and in pink striped shirt. She found that funny because it was too big on him, he was holding a lampshade. She placed the lavender ceramic back into the place, she noticed that it was the last piece on the rack. "It looks sad in grey."

She laughed or maybe it was a smirk. She didn't even know what sound she had just made. "I assume you have lamps at home?" she motioned towards his hands.

He chuckled, "well yes, obviously."

"You don't use the big lights?"

He looked sort of confused, "the big lights?" he had this smile on his face that was too nice to be for someone who's a stranger.

"You know the one that turns on when you click on a switch."

He chuckled again, "yes I do, but this one's for reading at night."

Her eyebrows perked up. "You read?" Not that it's amusing to know that he reads but that she didn't think of books when she was looking at the lamps, people use lamps to read books but then again, she wondered if the big lights were too big of a hassle to switch off after reading a book.

"Well, not really." He admitted, "I read sometimes."

"What do you read?" she asked. She did read, almost all the times. That was her only source of entertainment when she wasn't zoned out while she stared at the walls.

"Nothing interesting, I don't find them interesting."

"Then why do you read?"

"To fall asleep."

She laughed. Really laughed, "Understandable." For some reason he laughed too and there in the middle of *Decords,* they shared their numbers. He put his number on the receipt of the sad lavender plate, she didn't accept the plate at first but he insisted, he said "maybe this plate really wouldn't look sad if you looked at with happy memories, like today."

Even though the plate was worth three months of her travelling expenses and she didn't really know what to use that plate for, she nodded and took it. She noticed that the receipt was sprawled with a number and the name – Eden Nightstone. Pretentious name, she thought but he seemed too sweet to be pretentious so she smiled, "clever." And she gave her number written on a tissue paper from her college that she put in her pocket during lunch – Vienna Vittori.

"V.V?" he said smiling and for some reason she thought he called her Vivi, which didn't sound as bad.

After fourteen calls and thousands of texts later, it was officially a date and Vienna hasn't been on a date since her freshman year in college because she thought she lost interest in boys or any gender but then Carmy and Petal decided it was time for her to put herself out there and by out there they meant going on a date with Eden and she knew, Eden was different, he was charming, he seemed mature and he was *tall.*

"Do you think he's rich?" Carmy asked while she laid on her bed popping sour candy, "he looks cute, though."

"You really think he'd get her a five-hundred-dollar useless plate if he didn't have money?" Petal said while she laid left to Carmy, "That plate is ugly by the way."

Vienna sat below them, her back facing the bed, "I think that was the point of the whole ordeal, I'd say."

"He's rich," Carmy said again.

"Nobody cares if he is rich," Petal chimed in. "He can buy ugly plates but he cannot buy being a nice boyfriend."

"What is that supposed to mean?" Vienna said laughing.

"I think buying ugly plates is a part of being a nice boyfriend." Carmy sat up straight, "A great boyfriend, even."

"He is not my boyfriend," Vienne looked up at Carmy. "At least, not yet."

Petal scoffed while Carmy shrugged happily, "You like him."

"Of course I like him."

And she did, to her liking someone was a big deal. Like is the tip of the iceberg for her. Eden has been nice so far, she hasn't decided to fully like him but tip of the iceberg was enough for her and so she was there, in front of a sushi restaurant that she's been past a couple times while on her way to work, she's never been interested to go in but for some reason that was the first place that came to her mind when she was asked for a place to meet at.

She went in and her eyes instantly fell on Eden, he was wearing a pale blue shirt, oversized just like the other day and grey pants and a black watch that she couldn't tell the brand of. He waved at her and she smiled whilst she walked towards him, he tapped the seat next to his and she sat down. As she did that, she could instantly tell what cologne he was wearing – musk and cinnamon. She had the habit of recognizing people's colognes since she worked at one of those beauty store sections where they sell perfumes during her high school days.

"You look pretty," he said, under the yellow lights his cheeks seemed redder than usual, she couldn't tell if he was blushing or he was embarrassed.

She didn't dress up much according to the occasion, a plain black short skirt and a grey plain sleeveless top that kind of hugged her body in a way that she wouldn't wear it on a summer day paired with a single stoned chain from Petal and huge stoned studs that she got from the dollar store for an event long back, her red hair was a curly mess she couldn't seem to tame but somehow managed to make it stay put together.

While he ordered the sushi and talked about nothing, the silence was comfortable, for some reason she didn't want to break it.

"Is it good?" he asked while he was on the fourth roll of an Ebi Maki. Vienna nodded because her mouth was full of it, Eden laughed. It wasn't awkward, it was like she belonged right beside him in that sushi restaurant under the yellow lights, laughing.

CHAPTER III

Present

Vienna lay face down on her bed whilst Carmy caressed her hair, and Petal paced furiously around the room. As much as Vienna had dreaded this first meeting, her mind seemed to feel empty.

"You're telling me," Petal started, waving her hands around in her white satin set, anyone could tell she had rushed over straight from sleep. "You ran into that loser half-way across the globe when you haven't seen him once while living in the same city?"

It was a mystery Vienna herself had yet to solve. She had never taken any drastic steps to avoid Eden, yet she had never once seen him since their fallout. Now, of all places, she had run into him on an island—when all she wanted was to make peace with herself and support Petal at her wedding.

Vienna groaned and turned to face Carmy, who was smiling sadly as she held her belly. "Don't look at me like that."

"It's just, maybe something is meant to be with you guys." She looked at Petal helplessly, who just shrugged in disgust. "You running into him on his random island two years later is not a coincidence, because if you wanted to run into each other, it could've happened anytime."

Petal was furious but Vienna was confused in general, she didn't know what to think but she knew Carmel was the type of person to be positive about any given situation. She sat up straight and looked at Carmy, "I don't think it means anything, people vacation all the time."

She knew she was being truthful. If she had managed to avoid him for years while living in the same city, she could do it here too.

Carmy looked sad, Petal was shaking her head – Vienna couldn't really point out what face she was making. "Now, what are we having for lunch?"

They both looked at her in unison and then at each other. Petal sat next to them on the bed, "I don't know, honestly."

"I don't really want to eat right now," said Carmy. "I'm kind of full, but I think you guys should order in. We can put on a show and kind of stay in?"

Carmy looked pretty excited and what she recommended was also exactly what Vienna needed, Carmy always knew what she wanted at all times. Carmy was able to read her emotions in a way she couldn't do so to herself.

"That's a lovely idea," Petal agreed. "I get to choose the food; you guys can choose the show."

Vienna laughed and nodded, for some reason Petal had a peculiar palate, one that included not liking the food they always ordered.

After an hour, the food arrived and by that time they decided to watch the first *Sex and the City* movie which was mostly a pick by Carmy, they could not argue with her against it and Vienna wasn't really in the mood to pick a movie, she mostly wanted to sleep.

They ate the butter noodles and croquettes in silence whilst watching the part where Carrie throws her bouquet at Mr. Big in the middle of the street, she looked at Carmy who seemed so into it that her fork was halfway to her mouth.

She looked back at the screen, Carrie seems sad but she also knew Carrie always went back to Mr. Big no matter what so she kind of deserved it but it also made her think, was wanting to be loved a crime?

Carmy shook her head, "I can never believe he did that to her," she took a bite. "Who leaves a beautiful woman in her custom Viviene Westwood wedding gown right before getting married?"

"You're worried about her custom gown?" Petal asked laughing. "I feel like there's other things to worry about here."

"Like what?" Carmy chimed in.

"Like how she shouldn't be marrying this guy in the first place?"

Carmy rolled her eyes and went back to watching. But to Vienna, the food wasn't appetizing anymore. As she watched Carrie cry trapped in a love story that refused to let her go, she wondered if she was still caught in her own. She had made peace with the past. She knew that. She had repeated it to herself enough times for it to feel real. Yet, somehow, running into Eden again had stirred something she wasn't prepared for. It wasn't longing, wasn't regret. Just a quiet, nagging feeling that she couldn't quite name which was bothersome because she wondered if she had really come to terms with it or tucked it away at the corner of her mind hoping to never revisit.

Vienna pushed her food around on her plate, never taking a bite. She wasn't really paying attention to the movie either.

"Okay, what's up?" Petal's voice cut through her thoughts.

Vienna looked up, blinking as if she had just been shaken from a dream. "What?"

"You're zoning out. You haven't even touched your food."

Vienna glanced down at her untouched plate, the buttery noodles congealing under the dim hotel room lights. "I'm just tired," she said, but she could tell neither of them believed her.

Carmy sighed, set her fork down, and paused the movie. "You know, it's okay if this is messing with you a little."

Vienna shook her head. "It's not." It couldn't be. She had spent so long convincing herself that she had moved on, that Eden was a chapter closed so firmly it couldn't be reopened.

Petal scoffed. "You don't have to lie to us, Vie. You don't owe us that."

"I'm not lying," Vienna insisted, but even as she said it, she could feel the weight of the moment pressing in on her. The sight of him had unearthed something she thought she had buried for good. But maybe moving on wasn't about forgetting. Maybe it was about learning to live with the memories without letting them own you.

Carmy stretched out a hand, squeezing Vienna's wrist gently. "Whatever it is you're feeling, just... let yourself feel it. It doesn't mean you're stuck."

Vienna exhaled slowly. Maybe they were right. Maybe this wasn't about Eden at all. Maybe it was about making peace with the version of herself that had once loved him.

She finally took a bite of her food, picked up the remote, and pressed play.

CHAPTER IV

Past

Vienna laid on her couch, staring at the roof of her bedroom, wondering about the classes she has to attend in a couple of hours but had no energy to get up to. She wished to stay where she was and sleep for a couple more hours due to the lack of sleep from last night. Days seemed to be passing by slower when all she's doing is studying, which was gruesome because she did not particularly enjoy studying.

She contemplated not going to classes, but she knew she had to, so she got up and put on the nearest top – a fuzzy navy-blue sweater that she was sure she wore a couple of days ago; she had this weird habit of not washing her clothes unless it wasn't visibly dirty or smelled bad, which was probably a bad habit and she wanted to change it someday, but it didn't seem as concerning now.

On her way to classes, she considered getting a smoothie, but she really wasn't in the mood to eat anything either. She toasted up a couple of slices of bread and ate it on her way. As expected, the classes were exceptionally tiresome. By the time she got home, she wanted to crawl up into her bed and sleep again, but Carmy barged into her room, which wasn't all that surprising to Vienna since Carmy was more at her place than her own anyways.

"How were your classes?" Carmy asked while plopping up on her bed. She looked cheerful—she always was—but she seemed extra cheery.

"The usual," Vienna replied. "You seem happy," she asked, raising an eyebrow and smiling.

"Nothing," Carmy replied, her smile getting wider and brighter. "I just met a guy."

Vienna sat next to her. "Oh my god, who?"

"I'll tell you the details later," she said. "Can we go get something to eat?"

Vienna nodded, still smiling. She took her bag and let herself out of the house, followed by Carmy. On their way, Vienna noticed that the leaves had turned yellow. She hadn't noticed that—it was already fall.

When they reached the deli, Carmy grabbed cornbread and an espresso, and Vienna wasn't really in the mood to eat, so she decided to just get a mango milkshake. Carmy looked at it. "You're 20, you need to start drinking coffee."

"I don't really like coffee; it makes me barf."

They found a place to sit near a fountain crowded with pigeons. Vienna looked up at the trees again. "It's already fall."

Carmy looked up too. "It is," she sighed. "I don't like time."

Vienna now looked to Carmy. She had long eyelashes, and a couple of strands of her dark hair were sticking onto her lips due to her lip gloss. Carmy was such a pretty girl, even when they were young. She had a wide smile that lit up her whole face, and she was kind to everyone. Vienna didn't really know how to do that with people—she didn't know how to act like a person with other people. To her, she felt like a passing cloud. She didn't really know who she was or what to be with other people, and it was weird to think that she knew her friends more than herself.

"Who does?" she took a sip of her mango shake. It was like what one would expect—sweet, strong, and thick.

"It's like we were just thirteen, now suddenly we're twenty and having to make decisions for ourselves?"

Vienna understood where Carmy was coming from, but to her, she hasn't really made any life-changing decisions in her life yet. She goes to a normal school and works at a dog shelter. She doesn't really know what to do if she was being honest with herself. She's tried things her whole life, but unless she was exceptionally good at anything straight away, it didn't interest her. She did try being stagnant at roller skating once, but she knew she really wasn't built for that deep down, so she had to give that up. She was content with where she was at life.

"What happened with Eden?" Carmy asked, looking at her.

Vienna shook her head. "There's nothing much to say." Which was true. There was nothing to say. They hung out a couple of times, laughed till their stomachs hurt, and ate everything and anything that they could, but it was still that. She could feel a huge glow of radiance around herself when she was with him, but she didn't really know what to do with that feeling.

"He seems like a nice guy," Carmy said. "And I really mean that, not just for the sake of it."

"You wouldn't do that." She trusted Carmy and Petal way too much, so she'd take their word over anyone's any day. "By the way, where is Petal?"

Petal had been really busy with preparing for business school—she knew that—but she really hasn't seen her around in a while.

"Oh, I called her. She's busy with some applications."

Vienna nodded and went back to sipping her shake. The gentle breeze mixed with the scent of cornbread reminded her to take a bite out of it. She didn't really like it, but she ate it anyways. It was slightly getting darker. The group of pigeons now scattered into a few around the fountain, which seemed almost beautiful with the streetlights now bright and reflecting off of it.

Carmy stretched her hand out, sighing dramatically, "I wish I could stay twenty forever."

Vienna smiled, but something about that thought unsettled her. She wasn't sure if she wanted to stay twenty or if she just didn't know how to move beyond it.

CHAPTER V

Present

As Vienna tried to get into a peach-toned single-sided sleeve dress, Carmy shouted from the other dressing room that was next to hers, "I am too pregnant to fit into this."

"We can get it custom-made," Petal shouted from the main hall. "That's not a problem."

Vienna zipped up her back. The dress wasn't flattering at all. It did not match her tones and seemed so off-putting; the design in general was very odd. "Yeah, the problem is that this one's ugly." She swiped the curtains away and entered the hall to face Petal, who set her flute of champagne on the white table in front of her.

"You're right," Petal said slightly tilting her face to the side and scrunched up her nose.

"Carmy?" Vienna shouted. "Are you alright in there?"

Petal shook her head with her eyebrows raised. "You don't have to try it on. It looks ugly."

"Oh, thank god." Carmy came out with the dress in her hand. "I do not want to try on dresses. I will just see them on Vie and get them too."

Vienna nodded. "Makes sense."

"They do not make cute bridesmaid clothes for pregnant women; I'll tell you that."

Petal went back to sipping her champagne whilst Carmy sat down next to her. She looked tired, and Vienna wanted to tell her to get to her room to sleep, but this was for Petal's big day too, and she knew Carmy wouldn't listen to her either way.

Vienna went in with another yellow dress, which was given disapproving looks from both Petal and Carmy. As she tried on multiple other unflattering dresses, Petal was on the verge of calling it a day when she saw Carmy passing out on the couch, but Vienna noticed one of the store assistants pull a rack of clothes to the other section. She handed the dress she was holding to Petal and walked behind the assistant and tapped the girl on her shoulder.

The assistant turned back. *Amelie*—her name tag read.

"Hey Amelie," Vienna said, smiling to the girl who was much shorter than her. "I'm just wondering if this is the new collection?"

Amelie smiled. "Yes, this just came in."

Vienna felt a warm swarm of butterflies in her stomach. "This is perfect. Can I try these?"

"Of course," said Amelie, smiling widely. "I'll bring them to your hall."

Vienna nodded and went back to Petal and Carmy. Petal smiled at her. "Where did you run off to?"

"You'll see," Vienna smiled widely back at her and sat next to her. "We haven't done this since college."

"Yeah, we used to go to parties."

"You both went to the parties. I was dragged there."

"You enjoyed it." And she was right. She did enjoy them, mostly because she got to see Carmy go crazy with her dance moves while Petal failed miserably to flirt with her girlfriend. It's funny to think back because she is now marrying the said girlfriend, meanwhile Carmy is pregnant and asleep next to them. Vienna nodded and looked at the cream curtains. It used to be black at the department store they used to shop at, and it was tiny spaces where she could hear Petal breathe in the stall next to hers—not as big as a room with four stalls as this one.

Amelie came in with a rack full of clothes just in time. "I'll be right outside if you need anything." As she left, Petal stood up and looked through the clothes.

"You know what, Vie?" Petal said, grinning. "You did a great job running behind her. These are amazing pieces."

Vienna shrugged and stood up. "I'm trying the green one."

That dress was the reason she ran behind Amelie; it looked striking even from a long distance. She took it from the rack and went behind the curtains. She kept the dress on top of her and looked at it in awe under the warm lighting. She knew it'd be the perfect fit for both her and Carmy.

"Shut up," Petal shouted as Vienna came out in the long, straight-skirted emerald green dress. It had no sleeves, with just some sprinkled stones at the sweetheart neckline. The back was low, exposing her spine. She wasn't used to these types of dresses, but she loved this one and knew Petal would too.

"You like it?" she asked Petal while making a twirl.

"I love it," she said, waking Carmy slightly. Carmy stirred up and looked at Vienna. She gasped.

"This is lovely," she said, sitting up straight. "I think this is it."

Vienna nodded. "Do you want this same dress too?"

Carmy nodded. "Yes, but I'm getting this in powder blue. Green will not suit me."

Petal agreed. "We can customize it."

"Can you deal with these? I am going to my room," Carmy said, getting up. "Also, tell them to make this a halter neck for me. I cannot deal with a strapless dress right now."

Vienna gave a thumbs-up and went back in to change.

"Vie, can you give your measurements and Carmy's that she's given you? I need to go to the cake tasting. I'll pick up the bill later."

"Yes, sure," she shouted back. "You have fun."

She looked at her in the mirror for a second. Her red hair and the green dress really went well together. For a moment, she felt like she was in a different body in an alternate timeline where she doesn't have the random sadness that she always had within her.

Just as she was about to leave the store after giving Amelie the measurements and Carmy's requests, she noticed a familiar face at the counter. It was Eden. *Of course it is*, she thought.

Before she could avoid his eyes, he called out her name. Vienna waved awkwardly at him and smiled. She walked up to him because she either way had to pass the counter to the exit.

"What are you doing here?" he asked.

"Bridesmaid dress fitting," she said, shrugging.

Eden laughed lightly; it was the same laugh as before. Nothing has changed—not even him—and she was right back at where she was three years ago.

"I can't believe Petal is getting married."

"I know," Vienna said. "What are you doing here?"

"Picking up a suit," he said, and for a moment when he was looking at her, she saw a glimpse of what he really was trying to say. There was slight sadness in his eyes. Before she could fully process the moment, it was cut off by his phone ringing, and she quickly looked away.

He picked it up and whispered while she looked at the roofs of the shop to avoid the awkwardness. She could've left the store in this moment—this was her time to leave this interaction and get away from him—but she couldn't do that, so she just stood there and counted the panels.

"Hey," he said, and she looked back at him. "I need to leave, but we can have coffee sometime—or even ice cream for old times' sake?"

Vienna nodded, and he smiled.

"Great running into you in another country." And then he was gone, and it struck her that he's been thinking about her too—and that running into her in another country bothered him too.

Maybe there is something more to these unexpected run-ins than she has put the thought into.

CHAPTER VI

Past

The view from Eden's window was too dark. She realized it was already dawn and that she had to leave. She hadn't paid attention to the movie—nor had Eden, as far as she noticed. They paused the movie various times in between to talk, kiss, and eat, but that was pretty much it.

It was some slasher film that wasn't really interesting, and she knew Eden picked that on purpose. The fish and chips were now dry and stale. As she looked out the hall window from where her head rested on his lap, she realized it would take ages to live like him—in a penthouse on one of the highest floors and not worry about food drying up.

"You're telling me your parents are renting you this whole place just because you moved here for college?"

He laughed. "They own this place."

"Yeah, right," she said, looking up at him. "They just happen to buy places wherever they like?"

"Kinda?" he said reaching out for one of the dry chip.

"That must be nice."

"Who cares," he replied. "Once I get this degree, I'm getting out of their hair."

She was shocked at times, knowing he didn't really like his parents—especially when he came from a place that provided him with everything he needed instantly. She couldn't simply fathom that, ever.

"What will you do when you do leave?"

"I don't know, honestly."

She shook her head. "You'll figure it out."

"Hopefully."

She knew it was time to leave since she had an early day tomorrow, but she was too comfortable. She didn't want to sleep cramped up in her bedroom with the window left open for air. She wanted to wake up and go to his kitchen so she could "help" herself to some already made breakfast. Everything was to her liking—in a way that made her feel guilty about actually liking it.

As she laid there on his lap, she had a question she had to ask—because he'd never asked, and she'd never wanted to.

"Can I stay the night?"

Eden paused the movie. "I thought you'd never ask," he said, his eyes glimmering from the TV's light. "I thought you didn't feel comfortable here, so I never asked." He pushed her hair away from her eyes. "The answer is yes, obviously."

She smiled and nodded. "Can I change into something of yours?"

"You already know the answer to that too."

Honestly, she didn't know why she was awkward about this. She knew she liked him, and she knew Eden liked her too. They were aware of everything that was happening between them, but they'd never acknowledged what they were or put a label on it. Vienna didn't know if she wanted to put a label on it either—it was too scary, too much of a commitment. But she didn't know what was stopping Eden from asking.

"Do you actually want to watch this movie?" she asked, even though she already knew the answer.

He laughed. "No." He took up the remote once again, but this time to switch the movie off. "We can order in something else if you're hungry."

"I'm good," she said. "I'm too full, actually." Which was true—she ate too much in bits and pieces. Now her stomach couldn't handle anything that went beyond those small portions.

"You quite literally ate nothing," he said, pointing at the plate—half-eaten and dry. "I ate almost all of it. I feel bad."

"Nope, don't be. That is all I could eat."

Eden nodded as he caressed her hair. In that moment, she wanted to fall asleep right there on the couch, on his lap. She had felt a moment of peace this past noon—more than she had in her entire life. Which was weird, because the unfamiliarity was bothering her.

That made her realize something: to Eden, this is a comfort he's known his whole life. And anything out of this would be unfamiliar to him.

She knew she'd have this one day, but her mind simply couldn't wrap around this thought: some people go entire lives without ever recognizing their unfamiliarities.

CHAPTER VII

Present

As Vienna walked to the shores of the beach, she could see golden lights far away. She thought maybe they were the ships she'd see docking by the shores in the morning.

She dropped her shoes next to her and sat down. She hadn't been by the shore ever since she came to this island. She was content with seeing the waves from her windows in the room. For some reason, she liked seeing it from windows more than seeing it up close, and almost laughed at the thought of saying this out loud to Carmy and Petal. They'd say she had to get out more and meet more people—a concept she'd never quite got. What cause would that bring, exactly? But she also sometimes thought the complete opposite when she hung out with her friends. It was weird.

The way she could think in opposites depending on the people—her thoughts were a mirror of everyone she spent time with. People need other people. God forbid she wouldn't know what to do without Carmy and Petal, but since she's never needed anyone, she couldn't really grasp the idea of wanting people sometimes. They're necessary, but only to an extent.

The sound of waves crashing was crisper from nearby than when she was in her room. She thought about the last time she went to the beach—it was with her family on a road trip. The sand seeping into her toes made her queasy, and she'd never wanted to go back again.

The lack of sea in the city they grew up in was one of the reasons why Petal chose an island to spend the wedding month. She'd get two weeks, but a month had seemed like a nightmare when she first proposed the idea. All three of them had gone to the beach only a handful of times in their lives combined, so when Petal brought it up, she couldn't say no. It was her big day, and she'd do anything to make her feel special.

She wondered if the people living on the island were sick of the sea. As far as she'd seen, she hadn't noticed any natives—only tourists in bikinis with tan lines. Then again, she hadn't explored the island much to meet any locals.

She knew she was thinking too much for her brain to handle, but she also knew it was because of the sea. For some reason, when she looked at it, her thoughts raced. She could actually think. She wished she could lie down, but she wouldn't be able to see the waves crashing, so she rested her head on her arms over her knees.

For a while, she thought she was going to fall asleep, but the ship horns now and then kept her from doing so. She regretted not bringing anything to eat, but she ignored her craving and started staring at one of the ship lights, the one farthest from the group. That far out, the twinkling lights almost looked like stars. She settled into the thought that she was stargazing, in a way.

She heard footsteps and looked up to see a silhouette walking toward her. She couldn't make out who it was with the lack of light. As they came closer, she recognized Petal—her curly hair was a giveaway.

She waved at her and Petal waved back. When she reached Vienna, she handed her a box. It was hot, and Vienna placed it down next to her quickly.

Petal looked tired, like she'd just woken up. She wore a light green t-shirt she's had since high school. She wears it almost every day, as far as Vienna had noticed.

"That's food for you," Petal said. "I woke up to drink some water and saw you when I looked out my window."

Vienna looked back toward their rooms. They were pretty far but still visible. Their rooms were at the top and had a decent view of the sea.

"You could see me from there?"

Petal nodded. "I knew it was you because I didn't hear you come in next door, and no one else would come out to the beach at this hour."

Vienna nodded. "Thank you for the food. I was hungry."

"I know," Petal said.

Petal may not be as expressive as Carmy, but she had her moments—like this one. Vienna would even say Petal is the most loving person out of the three of them, but no one would believe it. Petal always seems stressed about something, which she usually is, but sometimes she's also like this.

"You can go back to sleep," Vienna said. "You didn't have to do this."

"Oh, I can't leave you in the dark like this on an island where we barely know people. Eat your food. I'll wait." She sat down next to Vienna, and all Vienna could do was smile a bit.

Vienna opened the box to find a sandwich and some fries with some kind of dip.

"Where did you even find this at this hour?"

Petal rolled her eyes. "We have room service."

Vienna shook her head. "I forgot about that."

"I did not spend this much on this bachelorette for you to forget," she said. "Use everything. They have a spa. You and Carmy should check it out."

"I will," she replied, taking a bite from the sandwich. It tasted heavenly—so much that she didn't even try to pick out what flavors or vegetables it had.

The view, the food, and Petal half asleep next to her made her realize this is why people need other people. It's possible to live without needing them, but they make life a little easier.

Just like the waves crashing on the shore, pushed forward by the next.

CHAPTER VIII

Past

Vienna wasn't really into art, but she put on the nicest dress she owned—a black satin one Carmy had gifted her for her eighteenth birthday—for the art show Eden had pleaded with her to attend. She rode with him, Eden dressed in a black suit, which was strange to see since she was used to him in t-shirts and college merch. It was refreshing to see him cleaned up. His blonde hair was slicked back in a way that made the shift from brown to blonde clearly visible. Usually, his hair was wavy and much fluffier—a mix of both colors.

"I don't know why I have to come to this art show," she said, slipping her feet out of the plain black heels. They were Petal's, a size too small, but Petal had insisted they'd fit perfectly. Vienna didn't usually wear heels, and she didn't have any that matched the outfit, so Petal had happily lent hers. But now her feet hurt, and she dreaded the next evening when she'd have to walk in them again.

"I told you," Eden said, steering the wheel, "all my friends will be there and you have to meet them."

Vienna nodded. She hadn't met his friends yet. It felt a little awkward, especially since they weren't officially anything, and he hadn't met Petal or Carmy either. She wasn't ready to bring up the "what are we" conversation—it was a stupid one anyway.

"I hope you have a good time," she said, looking out the window. She'd only agreed to come because of how excited he looked when he asked. The first time she brushed it off, but when he asked again, hugging her and refusing to let go until she said yes, she realized she was easy to convince—when it came to Eden.

When they arrived at the arthouse, Vienna was surprised by how grand the place was. She'd imagined some big white-walled house, but this looked like one of those palatial mansions from period films.

"This is huge," she said. "People show their paintings here?"

Eden laughed. "Paintings?"

"Isn't that what art is?" she asked, walking up the stairs hand in hand with him.

"You're right," he said. "But this isn't that kind of art."

Vienna was confused. She didn't really know much about art. She knew music, a few films and shows Carmy made her sit through, and books—for the most part. But this? "What kind of art is it?"

"You'll see," he said, winking. "Don't stress. You'll have a good time."

She wasn't stressed exactly. She just worried that when his friends started talking about the performance, she wouldn't know how to respond. She hated the idea of being the bystander in a room full of insiders.

Inside, the place was more extravagant than anything she'd imagined. Growing up in the same city as this "house" and never having seen it before felt surreal. But her circle had always been small. This was something else entirely.

The art Eden had mentioned turned out to be a performance—four people painted in different colors dancing in the main hall, repeating the same motions again and again. After one round, Vienna was done. She didn't really understand it, couldn't interpret it the way Eden and his friends did. He introduced her briefly, but she stood silently by his side while he chatted with them. Every now and then, he handed her a glass of champagne or a plate of food. He'd turn to talk to her about the performance, and she'd just nod and smile.

Looking around, everyone was dressed to impress and talking seriously—intensely. She didn't get what was so serious.

When it was finally over and he was helping her into his car, Eden leaned down and asked, "Do your feet hurt?"

She could smell his musk and cinnamon scent as he lifted the hem of her dress slightly, just enough to remove her heels. He pressed a small kiss just above her ankle.

Vienna sat there shaking her head, smiling as he closed the door for her.

When he got in on the other side, he said, "I know that wasn't very fun for you."

She leaned back in her seat and nodded. "It wasn't. I don't think your friends liked me."

"They just need some more time."

She didn't quite get that. People either liked someone or they didn't. They didn't need time to marinate. But she let it go—maybe people were different.

"Hey," he said, brushing his fingers lightly against her cheek. "This won't happen again. I promise."

She nodded again. She knew it wasn't his fault. It was just his circle, how he spent his time—and she simply didn't fit into that.

And she was okay with that.

CHAPTER IX

Present

The club music was so loud that even Vienna screaming at the top of her lungs to say anything to Carmy wasn't enough. She was concerned about her, but Carmy looked happy.

She pushed her way through the crowd, careful not to spill the drinks in her hands as she avoided flailing arms and bumping bodies. She let out a sigh of relief when she finally reached Carmy and Petal—Carmy swaying lightly to the beat while Petal was fully in dance mode.

Vienna handed Carmy her glass of water and gave the Long Island iced tea to Petal.

"I'm scared for you, Carmy."

Carmy took a sip from her glass.

"Oh, come on. This is probably the last time I get to go clubbing," she said, motioning to her baby bump.

"Yes, but you can go later," Petal added, her voice barely audible over the music. Surprisingly, she'd wanted to come to the club when Carmy insisted—partly to look out for her, but also because she felt like a hermit lately. She was trying to look on the bright side of being on vacation: no one here knew her.

"Absolutely not," Carmy gasped. "I don't want to be *that* kind of mother. No offense to the ones that do, but that's just not me."

"You're having a baby at twenty-four and Petal's getting married. You guys are way too young for this, in my opinion."

They both laughed.

"You're right," Petal said, downing her drink. "But it is what it is."

Vienna looked around the club—everyone sweaty, drinking, dancing on each other or doing all three at once. She decided to just stand where she was, next to Carmy, and people-watch. Petal had drifted into her own world, dancing slightly out of sight.

"I don't think I'm supposed to be here," Carmy said.

"Didn't you just say you had to do this *because* you might not be able to later?"

"You're right. But people are already looking at me weird."

"They're not," Vienna said. She'd noticed people in this club seemed to be in their own little worlds. Unless someone wanted to dance with you—or was the bartender—no one cared.

"They're not."

Carmy took another sip.

"You can dance in front of me," Vienna said. "Not too much, though."

"I'm not in the mood."

"It's okay. I won't be dancing either. We can just stand here sadly together."

Carmy laughed.

"Pregnancy has its downsides, I guess."

"Everything I've heard about it sounds like a downside."

Just as Vienna was admiring the neon colors splattered across the ceiling and walls, she scanned the crowd for Petal but caught sight of a dark-haired brunette instead—whose eyes met hers. Vienna immediately looked away.

She already knew the girl was coming over. Weirdly, she already knew *who* it was. And she didn't know why she kept running into people she knew on the other side of the world. It was starting to frustrate her.

"Vienna, do you know the girl beelining over here all cheery?" Carmy asked.

"Unfortunately, I do," Vienna said, finishing her appletini and placing the empty glass on the counter. "Hi, Nalia."

"How lovely to run into you on the other side of the world," Nalia said, all teeth and sparkly eyes—though maybe it was just the strobe lights.

Vienna gave her a faint smile.
"My friend's getting married."

"Oh, wonderful. I'm getting married too."

"Oh what?" Carmy said. "It really *is* the destination, huh?"

Nalia laughed. "Yes, it is. I'm Nalia Wern," she said, extending a hand. Her nails were done in blue and black tones, matching her navy-blue jumper with black stones near the collar and black knee-high boots. She was so put together it was almost blinding.

Carmy took her hand.
"Carmel Synclare."

"Carmel? Like the candies?" Nalia's face lit up again. "And you're expecting! I love babies. I can't wait to have one of my own someday!"

Behind her, Vienna spotted Petal approaching. Relief swept over her.
"Hey, Petal. Meet Nalia."

"The friend that's getting married," Carmy added. "Nalia's getting married here too."

"Oh, that's nice," Petal said flatly. "I need more drinks."

"Petal is a lovely name, by the way," Nalia said. "Vienna really surrounds herself with uniquely named people."

"How do you two know each other?" Carmy asked.

"Oh, you know. Around campus," Vienna said quickly.

Nalia nodded. "It's been so long. Nice meeting all of you—I have to run. I'll catch you guys later!"

She hugged Vienna, which caught her off guard, then vanished into the crowd. Vienna just stood there, confused by what had just happened—and already tired from the whole interaction.

"What kind of a fuck-ass name is Nalia?" Petal said. "Seems like a real character."

"She seemed nice," Carmy said, glancing at Vienna. "How come you never told us about her?"

"I have," Vienna said. "Remember the girl who said she couldn't punch my library card because I was three hours late returning a book?"

"Wait, *that's* her?" Petal's eyes widened. "Damn. She's getting married?"

Vienna wondered how many more people she was going to run into. She'd seen Nalia around the university library a few times, but they'd never been friends. Just small talk. Always smiling. Always polite.

Honestly, Vienna wasn't surprised she was getting married. But she didn't really get the point of marrying someone—even if you loved them. It seemed like too much of a commitment for your early twenties.

Maybe she was the miserable one all along. Even surrounded by joy, she stayed on the sidelines, watching it all and not knowing how to put herself out there—how to fit in effortlessly the way everyone else seemed to.

CHAPTER X

Past

The thrift store smelled like scented candles and old books. Carmy had already found her way to the small vinyl section and was flipping through records intently.

Petal held up a hideous dark blue sequined dress. "This is so you, Vie," she said, bringing it closer and laughing.

Vienna grabbed it from her and held it up to her body. "Very lovely, isn't it?" she said, twirling. "I should wear this at my graduation."

"Absolutely," Petal shot back, still laughing, before going back to the racks. "Seems like someone gave up their love for sequins. Everything here is so bedazzled."

Vienna was looking at the baby clothes. "Did someone give up on their baby too?" she said, holding up a bright yellow onesie.

"Hey, don't say that," Carmy chimed in. "The baby probably outgrew them."

Vienna put it down. "I didn't even think of that."

"People can outgrow things," Petal said. "That's insane to think about. One day you can just wake up and be like, 'Hmm, I don't like this anymore.' It's crazy."

"Well, you both aren't going to outgrow me. We're already too old for that."

"Nineteen does sound old," Carmy said. "I can't wait to be much older."

"I don't know if I want to be old," Petal said, pulling out a cream-colored top. She raised her eyebrows at it and put it back. "Well, I do, but I don't want to do adult things."

"I feel like you specifically are meant to be an adult," Vienna said. "You've always been a thirty-year-old woman stuck in this body. I actually want to see the thirty-year-old Petal in her full glory." Vienna meant it. Some people are built for the future. She wasn't sure if she was one of them.

"Thirty is not that old," Petal rolled her eyes.

The carpet under Vienna's shoes made a scratchy sound she kept rubbing her foot over. She picked up one of the candles and smelled it—it was rosewood, but almost empty. She turned it around to check the price: 60 cents. She put it back and picked up the vanilla one.

She wasn't planning to buy anything—she just wanted to look around. So did Carmy and Petal, but with the way they were studying items seriously, they might actually get something.

"Are we actually getting anything or just making the employees nervous?" Vienna asked, placing the vanilla candle back down.

"I might," Petal said, pulling out a silk scarf with a faint floral print. "This is cute, right?"

"If you were a 60-year-old French woman," Vienna said.

Carmy snorted, still flipping through records. "Vie is the least qualified to judge fashion. You almost just committed to that sequined nightmare."

"It would've been iconic," Vienna muttered, crossing her arms.

She turned back to the shelves, skimming over books stacked haphazardly. Her fingers landed on an old hardback—the spine faded, but the gold lettering still visible: *A Guide to the Moon and Stars*. She hesitated, flipping it open. Someone had scribbled notes in the margins.

She wondered who would find this book interesting enough to write in. Unless you were a preschooler just learning about the wonders of the universe, a guide to the moon and stars felt pretty useless.

She flipped to the last page, where someone had written: *Moon and stars are among us, if you look close enough.*

Vienna almost cringed, but she knew Carmy would find it poetic. Honestly, maybe she would too if she thought about it long enough.

She shut the book, shaking her head. *Moon and stars are among us, if you look close enough.* It was the kind of quote you'd find on a tote bag at an overpriced bookstore.

Still, she didn't put it back.

"Find something?" Carmy's voice came from behind her. Vienna turned to see her holding a record, the sleeve worn at the edges.

Vienna held up the book. "Look at this," she said, flipping to the last page. "Some wannabe philosopher left their legacy behind."

Carmy leaned in, reading over her shoulder. A slow smile spread across her face. "That's kind of beautiful."

Vienna rolled her eyes. "Knew you'd say that."

Petal appeared between them, peering at the book before glancing at Vienna. "You're buying it, aren't you?"

Vienna scoffed, clutching it to her chest instinctively. "I'm not."

Petal smirked. "You totally are."

Vienna opened her mouth to argue, but Carmy was already walking toward the register, the record in one hand and a new item in the other. "I'll get it for you," she said, tossing the book onto the counter.

Vienna groaned, following after her. "You're wasting a whole dollar on this."

"Sixty cents, actually," Carmy corrected. "A small bargain for a piece of the universe."

"Mind grabbing me this ugly scarf that costs thirty cents?"

Carmy shook her head and picked it up. Vienna noticed a baby headband pack in her other hand.

"Why are you getting that?"

"I don't know, it seems cute."

"You don't even have a baby."

"Maybe I will one day."

Vienna nodded. "You really don't have to get the stupid book though."

"Just think of it as a souvenir from today."

Vienna looked at Petal, who just shrugged.

She let out an exaggerated sigh but didn't fight it. The cashier rang everything up and slipped the book into a brown paper bag.

As they left the store, Vienna found herself running her thumb along the paper's folded edge. She wouldn't admit it, but a small part of her already wanted to read through every note.

CHAPTER XI

Present

The cake shop had a backyard that directly faced the beach. Vienna couldn't wrap her mind around how everyone in this town seemed to have easy access to the sea—whether they wanted it or not. She wondered how they managed natural disasters, if one ever struck.

"I don't know about the blueberry filling," Petal said, taking a bite of a cupcake. "It's too sweet for my liking."

Vienna picked up a cupcake next to the empty spot where Petal had taken hers and bit into it. The flavors hit her quickly—first the vanilla, then the blueberry filling, almost like jelly. Petal was right; it was too sweet.

"I don't think vanilla and blueberry go too well together," she said, taking another bite. "At least, not for you."

"What about the raspberry?" Carmy chimed in. "I think it looks good."

Carmy had cut back on sugar, so she mostly judged cakes based on appearance. She'd only agreed to taste the one flavor both Vienna and Petal approved of.

"Romy is allergic to raspberries, so that's out of the question."

"Why'd you order something your fiancée is allergic to?"

Petal wiped her hands on a tissue. "I just asked for all their flavors."

"How rich are you," Vienna asked, smiling and shaking her head. "Exactly?"

"Rich enough to pick the perfect cake for my wedding."

"What about this?" Vienna pulled the card closer. "Lavender honey cake?"

Petal took a bite. "Too wedding-y."

"But it looks nice," Vienna said. "Purple and cute."

"They can make any cake look nice," Carmy said. "It has to taste good."

"I feel like you can't go wrong with chocolate cake," Vienna weighed in. "It's rich and classic."

Carmy nodded. "I agree."

"But that's too normal," Petal argued. "We always had chocolate cake for our birthdays. I want something unique *and* tasty."

"What about this pistachio with rose buttercream?" Vienna asked, taking a bite. "This is thrilling."

"Pistachio gives off forty-year-old-woman-on-her-third-wedding vibes."

"Well," Carmy said, "we're never choosing a cake today."

Petal reached for the blueberry with lemon frosting cupcake. "Why are there like seven different types of blueberry cake?"

"People around here must love blueberries," Vienna said. "Maybe."

"I actually love this lemon frosting."

Vienna took a bite from the same cupcake as Petal, her eyes widening as the lemon hit her taste buds. "This is *actually* really good."

"Right?" Petal sighed. "Too bad the blueberry just doesn't work for me."

"We'll figure it out," Carmy said. "There's still a lot more."

And she was right—about fifteen other flavors were still left to try. Sometimes, the flavors blurred together, making it hard to tell one from another. No amount of coffee or water helped cleanse their palates. If it was good enough for Petal, only one part of the cake worked for her; otherwise, it was too bland. Vienna felt like she was dying a slow, sugary death—until she tasted the champagne cake with raspberry filling. It felt like something had brought her back to life.

"I think Vienna just saw God," said Carmy. "Look at her eyes."

"Petal," Vienna said. "You have to try this."

Petal took a bite and reacted the same way. Carmy lightly tapped the table. "It's raspberry. Don't get carried away."

"But Romy would *love* this champagne-flavored cake," Petal almost whined. "She'd be thrilled to have this at our wedding."

Vienna shook her head. She knew they'd probably need to start over again at another bakery until Petal found something perfect. But suddenly, an idea hit her.

"What if we combined the things you like?"

"Like what?"

"So far, you've liked the lemon frosting and the champagne cake. Why not mix them?"

"I'm calling the chef," Petal said, smiling. "Let's see what they can do."

After a ten-minute call—most of which Carmy and Vienna couldn't hear—it was official: the sample would be ready in a couple of hours.

"We can either wait here," Petal said, "or we can look around."

"I'm staying here. The sugar is getting to me," Vienna said, slouching in her chair. The sun was setting, making the waves sound softer, more serene.

It felt like everything was winding down. Carmy had already dozed off. Petal was walking by the water, sunglasses still on in the dark. Vienna just stared at the sky. They could've headed back to their rooms, but she knew how important this cake was to Petal—they had to be here for her.

A few minutes later, the chef arrived. She was a blonde woman with striking blue eyes, someone who looked like she belonged in a food magazine.

"I was closing up, so I brought it to you myself."

Vienna waved Petal over. Petal walked toward them, sunglasses still on.

"You didn't have to come all the way, Kiara," Petal said.

"Oh no," Kiara replied. "You've waited long enough. Here's your cake: *Champagne Dreams with Lemon Chiffon.*"

Vienna tapped Carmy's shoulder, waking her instantly.

"Oh—the cake's here," she said. "You made this?"

Kiara nodded. "I'm the head pastry chef."

"That's wonderful."

"I love the name," Vienna said. "Of the cake."

"Yes, we name them all. They're like my babies."

Vienna nodded. "Makes sense."

"Please, have a bite."

Each of them picked up a cupcake and bit in. Vienna instantly knew—the lightly fruity bitterness paired with the sharp citrus hit of lemon was *exactly* what Petal had been looking for.

Petal grinned. "This is amazing."

Kiara laughed. "I'm glad."

"This is exactly what I wanted."

Carmy nodded, still savoring the flavor. "I think you've found your wedding cake, Petal."

"Yes," Petal agreed. "I have."

CHAPTER XII

Past

"The tall blonde has a cabin by the lake," Petal mocked, dragging her suitcase from the back of the car. "What's next? A mansion in the city?"

Vienna shrugged. Petal's eyes widened. "I *knew* this guy was loaded when he got you that ugly plate, but not *this* loaded."

Carmy walked around from the other side of the car. "Money isn't everything. Is Vie happy?" she asked, gently rubbing one side of Vienna's arm with a smile.

Vienna nodded. "I am," she said, moving toward the trunk. "You *knew* he was rich. Why is this shocking?"

"Rich and *rich*, Vie. There's a difference," Petal said, slamming her suitcase shut. "Next, you're going to tell me his last name is something ridiculous like—"

"Nightstone," Vienna muttered.

Petal froze. Carmy blinked.

"You're joking."

Vienna sighed. "I wish."

Petal burst into delighted laughter. "*Eden Nightstone*—oh my God. That's not a real name. Did you snatch him from one of those badly written fanfics online?"

"It's pretentious," Vienna admitted. "Sounds like he should own a company that manufactures expensive pens."

"Or a yacht," Carmy added, finally amused.

"Or a castle," Petal said. "I bet if we Google him, there's a Forbes profile just waiting."

"Lucky for me, he's not on that level," Vienna groaned. "Yet."

"He's a real character," Petal said. "Isn't he?"

Vienna waved her off. "He's nice."

"I agree," Carmy chimed in. "From what I've heard, he sounds like a nice guy."

"I'll be the judge of that," Petal said, rolling her suitcase behind her.

The air was slightly chilly. Vienna wished she had worn a coat, but they were already at his house. She walked past Petal and knocked on the door. It opened instantly, like he'd been waiting.

Eden's blonde curls were a mess. He looked like he'd just woken up—grey sweats, hoodie sleeves pushed up. He pulled Vienna into a hug. He still smelled like soap, so she knew he'd only recently gotten out of the shower.

"Come on in," Eden said, taking both Petal and Vienna's bags. "I'll get yours in a second," he told Carmy.

Petal raised her eyebrows at Carmy, who just shrugged when Eden turned around.

"I'm Eden," he introduced himself. "You must be Carmel. And you're Petal, right?"

"On spot," Petal nodded.

"Take a seat," he said, gesturing toward the couch. "What do you guys drink?"

"I'll take wine," said Petal.

"I'll take coffee," said Carmy at the exact same time.

Vienna laughed as Eden looked momentarily confused.

"We can drink later," Vienna offered.

"Fine with me," Petal said. "But driving for five hours nearly killed me. I *need* alcohol in my system."

"It *is* pretty far out," Eden admitted. "I'm sorry."

"Not a problem," Petal said. "We've never been to a cabin before. I took my chances."

"Oh really?"

"Yeah, we've been to a lake at best."

"Well, you're free to come here anytime."

A couple of hours passed—napping, sipping drinks (mostly Petal), and wandering around. Carmy wanted to explore the house. Vienna offered to tag along, but Carmy insisted on going alone.

Vienna didn't feel entirely comfortable yet. The cabin was *too* well put together. She was scared to touch anything; afraid she might misplace something. It felt like if even one thing was moved, it'd be obvious she didn't belong. She sank into the couch cautiously, trying not to move too much. Even the couch felt stiff, almost plastic, like it refused to soften for her.

Eden pulled her closer. "You're cold," he said, standing. "There are spare jackets upstairs—take whichever you want."

Vienna hesitated. The last time she borrowed one of his jackets, it had smelled like his cologne—one she couldn't even pronounce—and she hadn't been able to wear it without feeling like an imposter.

"I'm fine," she said instead.

"I'll get you a blanket. You look tired. I'll wake you for dinner."

Vienna nodded, watching him disappear upstairs. The warmth of his hand on her arm lingered longer than it should have.

"He *is* sweet," Carmy giggled. "I can't think of one reason to hate him."

Vienna smiled. Suddenly, the couch didn't feel quite so stiff. She could breathe again.

The house was quiet for a moment, only the faint sound of Eden's footsteps above. Vienna let her eyes drift shut, exhaustion finally catching up to her. The couch, it turned out, was *too* soft. Softer than her own bed—despite the six months she'd saved to buy it.

Maybe comfort *does* come at a higher price, she thought.

She wondered: if the couch was this soft, how soft would Eden's bed be? Did people like him even think twice before getting the best things for a house they barely used?

The thought struck her again—the couch might be softer than Eden's arms. Ironic, considering she'd always believed being with him would be the safest place to land.

"Comfort comes with the highest price," she thought again.

She knew she shouldn't think like that.

But she did.

CHAPTER XIII

Present

Petal had gathered them to put together the guest list. Vienna wasn't really in the mood—she didn't know many people, even if Petal insisted they all hung out around the same group.

"Don't you think it's too much to get people we barely know flown in here?"

"That's why we're putting together a list," Petal said. "To fly in people who actually deserve to be at my wedding."

"It's not like we all went to the same college," Carmy agreed with Vienna. "We don't know who you're expecting us to put on your wedding list."

"You're right," Petal admitted. "I should do this with Romy instead."

"Yeah," Vienna said. "I'm going back to my room."

"But you guys can invite anyone if needed."

"I'm too tired. I'll think about it tomorrow," Carmy said.

"Carmy, aren't you supposed to be doing doctor visits?" Vienna asked, raising her eyebrows. "You've been too tired lately."

"My doctor's all the way back in the city," Carmy replied. "Plus, I already asked if I'm okay to be traveling, so yeah, no worries."

"But if you feel like you need to see a doctor, there's probably one on the island," Petal offered. "I'm sure."

"Yes, of course. I'm aware."

Vienna knew Carmy was more hyper-aware of her health than she and Petal combined, so she didn't have to worry—but she still looked out for her.

Vienna stretched her arms as she made her way back to her room, already feeling the weight of the day settle in. She wasn't sure why she felt so drained—it wasn't like she'd done much besides sit around while Petal tried to organize the guest list. Maybe it was the constant reminder that this was really happening—that they were actually here, days away from Petal getting married.

She kicked off her sandals and collapsed onto the bed, staring at the ceiling.

A knock at the door made her groan. "I'm sleeping."

"That's a lie," Carmy's voice came through. "You always take at least an hour of doing nothing before you actually fall asleep."

Vienna sighed, sitting up. "Fine, come in."

Carmy pushed the door open, holding two glasses of iced tea. "Figured we could use this. Petal's still in wedding mode, so I escaped."

Vienna took one of the glasses and scooted over to make room on the bed. "She's going to be unbearable until the wedding's over, isn't she?"

Carmy laughed, tucking her feet under her. "Completely. But it's kind of sweet, isn't it? Seeing her like this? We always knew she'd be the one to get married first."

Vienna hummed in agreement, watching the condensation trail down her glass. "No, I always thought it'd be you first," she said. "But you skipped all that and went straight to the baby." She smiled, glancing at Carmy's belly.

They sat in silence for a few moments, the morning air filtering through the open window. It was calm, peaceful—a rare pocket of quiet between all the wedding chaos.

"Do you think you'd ever have a wedding like this?" Carmy asked, swirling the ice in her drink.

Vienna snorted. "Absolutely not. Too much planning, too many people."

Carmy grinned. "Figured. You'd probably elope and send us a postcard after."

Vienna tilted her head, considering it. "That doesn't sound so bad."

They laughed, and for the first time that day, Vienna felt lighter. "But I don't think I'd get married at all."

"Why's that?" Carmy asked, taking a sip.

"That just isn't me," she said. "I've never felt like I'd be someone's wife."

Carmy nodded. "Me too. But I knew I'd always have a family."

"And you're already halfway there."

Carmy smiled, swirling the ice again. "Yeah, I guess I am."

Vienna leaned back against the pillows, watching her. "Do you ever feel scared?"

"Of what?"

Vienna hesitated. "Of how everything's changing. Of... stepping into something you can't undo."

Carmy exhaled, setting her glass on the nightstand. "I'd be lying if I said no. But I also think that's part of it, right? You can't know everything before it happens. You just have to hope you're making the right choice."

Vienna traced the rim of her glass. "That's exactly what terrifies me."

Carmy hummed. "Not knowing, or not being able to leave once you do?"

Vienna didn't answer right away. She wasn't sure. Maybe both.

She stared at the ceiling, listening to the faint hum of the ocean. The room was dim, the bedside lamp casting soft shadows. Time felt slower here, stretched thin in a way that made it easy to get lost in your own head.

Carmy bumped her shoulder lightly. "You know, you don't have to have it all figured out."

"I know," Vienna said with a sigh. "But it feels like everyone else does."

Carmy laughed softly. "Trust me, we don't. Petal's just good at pretending. I'm just rolling with it."

Vienna glanced over. "And me?"

"You?" Carmy smirked. "You overthink everything, then act like you don't care."

Vienna rolled her eyes but smiled. "Annoying that you know me so well."

"Someone has to."

The room fell into a quiet comfort, broken only by the distant waves. Vienna exhaled slowly, letting herself sink into it.

Carmy stretched her arms overhead. "Alright, I should probably head back before Petal thinks I bailed on her permanently."

Vienna nodded, watching her pick up her half-empty glass.

Before she left, Carmy turned, a soft smile on her lips. "You don't have to know if you'll ever want to get married, Vienna. But whatever happens—you'll always have us."

Vienna didn't say anything. But as the door clicked shut behind her, she let out a breath.

Maybe that was enough. At least for now.

CHAPTER XIV

Past

Vienna stared at herself in the mirror. The light blue, long-sleeved dress was hugging her body in a way that was triggering her sensory issues, but she wanted to look good tonight. She felt like it was the perfect opportunity to feel good about herself in a dress she'd been avoiding for so long, and the date with Eden seemed like the perfect fit to wear it out.

Just as she was about to walk out the door, she heard the horn and instantly knew it was Eden. She opened the door and looked at him. He had his windows down and waved at her. She opened the door and got into the seat next to him.

He hugged her. She could smell his freshly sprayed cologne.

"You look beautiful," he said, rolling the windows up.

"So do you," she said. "Where are we going?"

"You'll see."

"It better not be one of those places that will serve us a spoonful of pasta and max out your card."

He laughed. "Don't worry about that."

"I worry a lot," she said, putting on her seatbelt.

As they drove to the place, the radio played music that was barely audible, but it was filling up the silence. Vienna felt uncomfortable in her outfit. She wanted to take it off as soon as possible, but she did choose it to look good, so she was stuck in between.

Vienna shifted slightly, adjusting the hem of her dress. The fabric still clung too tightly, but she tried to ignore it. She had chosen this dress because it made her look good, because she wanted to feel beautiful tonight. Still, a part of her regretted it—the sensation was gnawing at her, making her restless.

Eden glanced at her out of the corner of his eye. "Are you cold?"

She shook her head. "Just... trying to get comfortable."

He reached for the AC dial and turned it slightly. "Better?"

"Not really," she admitted.

"Are you not feeling well?" he asked. "We can just do this later."

"What?" she asked. "No, no, I feel good."

The road stretched ahead of them, dimly lit by streetlights that flickered between patches of darkness. Vienna let her gaze drift, the passing buildings and neon signs blurring into soft streaks of color. The music from the radio hummed quietly in the background, and for a while, neither of them spoke.

She liked it like this—the quiet moments where they didn't have to fill the air with words.

Then the car slowed down, and Eden pulled into a narrow street lined with cozy, candle-lit restaurants. Vienna glanced out the window, her brows raising slightly. The place looked expensive, with a line of valet drivers waiting at the curb.

She shot him a look. "I thought I told you no overpriced pasta."

Eden smirked but didn't say anything as he parked the car. He turned to her, his eyes shining under the warm lights. "Trust me?"

Vienna exhaled dramatically. "Not really."

"You okay?" he asked, watching her carefully.

She hesitated, then nodded. "Yeah."

Eden didn't seem convinced, but he let it go, reaching for her hand as they walked toward the entrance. Vienna let him take it, but she could already feel herself focusing too much on the sensation—the warmth of his palm, the slight pressure as he intertwined their fingers.

Inside, the restaurant was dimly lit, the golden glow of hanging bulbs giving the space an intimate feel. There were only a handful of tables, most of them filled with couples leaning in close, whispering over glasses of wine. The place smelled like fresh basil and something rich—like truffle, maybe.

Vienna bit the inside of her cheek. "So this is what we're doing tonight?"

Eden grinned, handing the host his card before she could argue. "You'll like it."

She huffed, crossing her arms as they were led to a small table by the window. She wasn't used to places like this—where the air felt heavy with elegance, where the waiters spoke softly and moved effortlessly, where people probably spent half their rent on one meal.

Eden, on the other hand, looked completely at ease. He sat back, relaxed, scanning the menu like this was just another Tuesday night for him.

Vienna glanced at her own menu, her stomach twisting slightly.

"Are you actually going to eat?" Eden asked, "or are you going to complain about the prices the whole time?"

"I might do the latter while I eat," she said. "You'd be surprised at my multitasking skills."

He laughed, setting his menu down. "How about this: I pick the food; you pick the dessert?"

Vienna considered it. "Fine. But if you order anything weird, I'm not touching it."

"No raw seafood. Got it," he said, smiling while closing the menu.

Their server returned, and Eden ordered for them both. Vienna only half-listened, too focused on the restaurant itself—how different it was from the places she usually went. The low hum of conversation, the quiet clink of silverware against porcelain, the way the candle on their table flickered every time someone passed.

She reached for her water glass, tapping her fingers against the stem.

Eden leaned forward, resting his arms on the table. "You're overthinking."

Vienna raised an eyebrow. "About what?"

"Everything."

She scoffed. "That's dramatic."

Eden tilted his head, watching her. "Not really. You're uncomfortable in that dress, you don't like fancy restaurants, and you're probably wondering if I spent too much on this meal already."

Vienna shook her head. "They're all valid reasons to overthink."

"It's one day," he said. "You'll be fine. Relax."

And she knew that. She was trying to do that. But she just felt so out of place, too distracted to focus on anything that was going on.

She sat back, exhaling. "Well, maybe I wanted to dress up for once."

"I'm not saying you shouldn't," Eden said, his voice softer now. "I just don't want you to feel like you have to."

Vienna stared at him for a moment. There was something about the way he said it, like he actually meant it. Like he really saw her.

Before she could respond, their food arrived—plates of freshly made pasta, rich with sauce and herbs, the scent immediately filling the space between them.

Vienna picked up her fork, twirling a small bite. "If this sucks, I'm never letting you order for me again."

Eden grinned. "Deal."

She took a bite.

It was good. Annoyingly good.

Eden raised an eyebrow. "Well?"

Vienna chewed slowly, dragging out the suspense. "I guess... it's edible."

He laughed, shaking his head. "You're the worst."

They ate, talking about nothing and everything—about the new book Vienna was reading, about Eden's failed attempt at learning how to cook, about the ridiculousness of overpriced restaurants and how Vienna could never take them seriously.

By the time dessert arrived, a small chocolate tart with a perfectly glossy top—she felt lighter.

Eden handed her a spoon. "Your turn to decide if this place is worth it."

Vienna took a bite, closing her eyes dramatically. "Okay. Fine. This part I approve of."

Eden leaned back, satisfied. "I knew I'd win you over eventually."

Vienna rolled her eyes, but she couldn't take any of this seriously. "I don't know," she said. "This feels wrong."

"Why would it feel wrong?"

"I never asked you for any of this," she said, putting her spoon down, the dress now getting itchier.

"You don't have to ask me for all this," he said. "I do it because I want to."

"But who am I to you for you to want to do all this? It's not like I am your girlfriend." She wished she could swallow up her words like she did with the food just a couple minutes ago, but it was too late now.

Eden put his spoon down too, but audibly louder than hers. She knew that wasn't what he meant to do, but it was all the more nerve-wracking to hear it.

"Vienna, yes you are. I love you, that's why I am doing this."

Vienna shook her head. "What?"

"What?" Eden asked, confused.

"What did you just say?"

"I said what I said," he replied, picking up his spoon again. "I wanted to say it earlier but I didn't know how."

"Well, definitely don't say it during an argument?"

Eden nodded. "Sorry, I didn't know we were arguing."

"No, you're not," she said, scoffing.

"Yes, I am not sorry for saying I love you during an argument."

Vienna shook her head. "You don't have to take me out to these expensive places like all the time."

She was weirdly aware of the dynamics—the dress that made her feel uncomfortable and a bill that was coming their way that Eden would definitely pay without looking at the price. She felt detached, and she was very much aware of the fact that she let his "I love you" hang in the air like that.

She knew she had a long way back to her home.

CHAPTER XV

Present

Vienna decided to take a walk around the island and explore on her own. She thought she'd take along Carmy, but she already seemed tired enough, so she let her sleep and came out on her own.

Her white tank top and long white skirt seemed appropriate enough to wear out since the sun was out and scorching, but she thought maybe she should have swapped out her skirt for a pair of denim shorts as she walked out a couple steps from her hotel—but it was too late.

She got herself a tender coconut to drink since she didn't remember to bring out her water bottle. As the coconut water hit her parched tongue, a bit too salty and sweet, she muttered out a "thank you" and continued her walk.

There were beaches everywhere, as usual. People seemed to have doubled up in quantity ever since she arrived. She could tell almost none of them were locals.

As she made her way to the market—which, to her surprise, was less crowded considering that it was a weekend—there were all kinds of stalls, from readymade food to raw vegetables and meat.

There was a bunch of jewelry shops on the next lane. She thought to stop by a couple to maybe get matching bracelets for her, Petal, and Carmy. She eyed each one while sipping on the coconut water. Some had dreamcatchers hanging out by the entrance, some had paintings, and for some reason, she noticed that the ones selling paintings were much more crowded than the others.

She finally spotted a stall with colorful beads laid out at the front and walked towards it. The beads sparkled under the sun's rays, and she noticed the variety of charms laid right next to them. She almost smiled to herself, knowing that Carmy would've loved to see this too.

"Do I get to pick out the beads?" she asked the woman who seemed to be in her mid-fifties, sitting on the right. She seemed to be putting together blue and yellow crystals—Vienna wasn't sure what she was making.

"Yes, honey," she replied, smiling. "You get to pick both the beads and the charms."

"How much do they cost—" she began, but she didn't hear the response because she was cut off by another voice behind her.

"Vie?"

She knew all too well whose voice it'd be. She took a deep breath in and turned around with a smile.

"Hi, Eden?" she said. "What are you doing here?"

He laughed. "I came here to look around."

She nodded and noticed that his hair was now almost all brown with streaks of blonde—just the opposite of how she last remembered it. She wondered if that's something that happened with age, but he looked like he hadn't aged a day since she last saw him.

"I was looking around too."

"Find anything interesting?"

"Yeah, actually—this charm bracelet," she said, pointing to them. "They look cute."

"Oh, that's great," he said. "We can't seem to find anything."

Behind him, she noticed a familiar face. She looked closer to see Nalia walking their way, smiling too big. She had her sunglasses on the top of her head and her hands full of bags. She brought them up to give a very struggled wave.

Vienna smiled a little and waved back. Eden squinted and looked back and forth between them. "You know her?"

"Yeah, barely."

"Oh wow," he said. "That is going to make things awkward."

"What? Why?"

Vienna was confused, but it disappeared once Nalia hugged her.

"I love running into you," she said. "Love familiar faces from back home that isn't just Eden."

"You know him?"

Nalia laughed loudly, and Vienna just looked at her, not knowing what to say. "What happened?"

"Know him? You're silly," she replied. "I am marrying him this month."

Vienna opened her mouth, but words didn't really come out. She turned that into a smile—a huge one that she wouldn't normally do. She looked at Eden, who didn't seem that thrilled—or he looked sad. She couldn't really distinguish the look on his face.

"Well," Vienna said, gripping onto the coconut, which she was hyperaware of now, holding it. "Congratulations to you both. So happy for you guys."

"Thank you," Nalia said in a voice that was almost a singsong. "You should come."

Vienna clicked her tongue. She didn't know why she did that but played it off. "I'll try to. My best friend's getting married too."

"Oh yeah, Petal, right?"

"Yep." She looked back at Eden, who still had that weird look on his face. She wondered if it was guilt.

"How did you guys meet?"

"Oh, same as you," Nalia said, putting her shades down. "At the library."

"Surprising," she replied. She knew Eden hated the library—he even hated reading books that weren't a part of his coursework. So that was odd.

"It is a funny story actually," she said. "He came to return books of someone who was way past their due. I just don't remember who it was."

Nalia looked at Eden. "Do you remember, Ed?"

Vienna almost laughed at the nickname she called him, but she swallowed it back and smiled. "Yeah, do you remember?"

Eden shook his head. "Nope."

She knew that Eden remembered. Those were her books—the books that he left at his place that she was never able to retrieve back. She thought they were a lost cause, so she decided not to go back to the library anymore and had to switch to the one that was thirty minutes away from her place.

"Well," Vienna said. "I guess I'll see you guys around. I have to get back to Petal."

"Oh, come grab lunch with us," Nalia said. "You look hungry."

"No," she said. "I'm fine. Maybe later."

Nalia nodded and waved back. "You definitely need to hang out with us later."

"Sure."

Vienna's walk back to her room felt painfully slow. She sipped from the almost-empty coconut—now too warm, the sweetness faded.

The conversation replayed in her head: the way Eden had said *nope* too fast, the way she could never hate Nalia, who seemed like the inventor of kindness.

But none of that mattered.

The only thought that truly stuck—one that hit harder each time it resurfaced—was that she had been nothing more than a bridge in his life.

A step toward his final, forever person.

CHAPTER XVI

Past

Petal took off the comforter from her bed and shook it off, the dust flying off clearly visible from the sunlight pouring in from the window.

Carmy was sat by the bed, swatting the dust off her face. "I just can't believe you didn't say it back," she said, looking at Vienna, who was laid down flat in Petal's room, the carpet poking into her black-and-white striped t-shirt—but she didn't want to get up. "Especially when you clearly do."

Carmy was right. It was bothering her, but she simply didn't want to say it then. It almost felt like she was obliged to say that she loves him because he took her out to a fancy dinner—but she'd never admit that to her friends, because she knew they'd talk her into saying it wouldn't feel that way. But they won't get it. They weren't there, and she didn't know how to put it into words in a way they'd understand.

"You guys weren't there," she rolled to the side where she couldn't face them. "He said it while we were arguing."

"All the more reason to know that he actually means it," Petal said. Vienna could hear her ruffling the sheets. "People don't just slip out I-love-you's unless they mean it."

"I have seen it," Carmy said, nodding. "He does love you."

"I know he loves me. It's just the way he said it."

"You can't dissect that one situation," Petal said. "Imagine how he probably feels—you didn't even say it back."

"Hey," Vienna said defensively, turning back. "You're supposed to be on my side."

"I *am* on your side," she shot back. "I'm just saying—"

"You should talk to him," Carmy cut her off. "You should just talk to him."

Petal nodded, pursing her lips. "I do agree with Carmy—just talk to him."

"He's been acting like nothing happened," Vienna said. "I don't think he wants to talk to me."

Vienna was looking forward to what he'd say later on, but he never brought it back. It was like how they were before the whole fiasco happened, and she didn't know how to bring it up when he seemed so unfazed by it.

"Of course he wants to talk to you," Carmy said. "He probably didn't bring it up because he didn't want to make things awkward for you."

"I'll try talking to him," Vienna said, sighing. "Do you guys think I should go up to his house now?"

"I mean," Petal looked up at her roof for a moment and then looked back at Vienna. "Yeah. You both need to get out of my room if you're not going to help with cleaning."

"Yeah, I am leaving," Vienna said, getting up.

"I will help you," Carmy said. "I don't have anything to do anyway."

"You guys have fun," Vienna said. "I'll come help if I finish up early."

"You won't—don't bother coming."

Vienna waved and left her house. She had to catch a bus to reach Eden's house. She knew he'd be home around this time, but she'd never shown up unannounced at his place before.

The travel to his house was quiet. There was barely anyone on the bus. She looked at the trees passing by—it was almost winter, and the air was getting colder day by day. Vienna felt like only the seasons had changed, but her life not so much, which wasn't really something she was expecting a change in anyway. She had no dreams, really. She was content with what she had because she didn't really know what she wanted in her life to change. She liked that the seasons changed, but she didn't really know if she'd be happy with one in her life.

The door to Eden's apartment had bright red paint all over it. The knocks on it sounded almost like a hammer hitting. She never really liked it—the color or the sound. She'd even mentioned it once to Eden, but he didn't really care about the color of the door unless he had a house behind it.

Eden opened the door half-asleep; he yawned before he could recognize it was Vienna and croaked out a very silent, "Hi, what are you doing here?"

Vienna didn't really reply. She walked past him into the house. He shut the door behind her.

"Put your coat on, we're going out."

Eden looked at her, puzzled. Vienna eyed his coat. "Okay, okay."

After ten minutes, they were out of his place and by the market. Every place seemed to have only a handful of people around. Vienna liked it when people weren't around in her town. It was the cold, but she knew they'd be out by the evening again.

Eden walked by her side, still puzzled. "What are we doing?"

"Don't ask questions."

"Okay," he smiled. "I won't."

She looked around, like she was looking for someone. When her eyes finally landed on the churro cart, her face lit up and she ran toward it, grabbing onto Eden.

"Two churros please," she said and looked at Eden, who reached into his pocket.

"Nope, this is on me," she said, swatting his hand.

Eden put up his arms in surrender. "Fine by me," he said. "Just this once."

Vienna wasn't really listening while grabbing the hot churros from the lady who sells them. She smiled and muttered out a "thank you."

She pushed one set of it into Eden's hand, who almost let it slip from the abrupt act, but he acted quick and caught them before they could touch the ground.

"That gave me a heart attack," Vienna said. "Thank God."

"Don't worry about it," he said, as his eyes fell onto a public bench. He fast-walked toward it and wiped it off with his coat sleeve. "Come sit here," he motioned to Vienna.

As they sat next to each other and indulged in the hot churros and chocolate sauce, Eden was thrilled to be biting into it.

"This is amazing, Vivi," he said, mouth full. "So fucking delicious, my God."

Vienna laughed at the chocolate sauce dripping down his chin. She wiped it off with her index finger and licked it away instinctively. "This cost like four dollars, by the way," she said.

"You're joking?"

"I am not," she said. "I've been coming here since I was like three years old just for their churros."

"I can see why," he said. "I've never had anything like this in my life."

Vienna looked at him, as she took in the moment of him enjoying a tiny bit that was a part of her life and how much he seemed to like it.

"I love you too," she said.

Eden stopped chewing and looked at her, his mouth still full. Vienna smiled, her eyes glistening. She realized that she seemed to be smiling when she was with him a lot—her cheeks seemed to always hurt when she went home after spending time with him.

"This is the best fucking day of my life," he said and hugged her. Churros and all.

Vienna held onto his arm that was around her back.

"I do mean it," she said. "You said it your way, I wanted to say it my way."

He pulled back and looked at her. "That was not how I wanted to tell you. It just slipped out."

"I know," she said. "I still liked it though."

Eden laughed. "I love you," he said. "And I love these churros."

Vienna laughed along with him. "I love Eden and these churros."

Under the setting sun and gathering crowds, by a small churro shop that people would miss if they walked by too fast, Vienna had a glimpse of what she may want. She wanted to see Eden happy, she realized. And she wanted her cheeks to hurt when she went home. She wanted to travel by bus from her friend's place and make life happen.

She realized her dream was just to live.

CHAPTER XVII

Present

"I just can't believe he's getting married," Carmy said, scrolling through her phone. "To Nalia, at least."

"Why? She seems nice," Vienna said, twirling the thread that was poking out of the cushion she was sitting on. "I'm happy for him."

"We're all happy," Petal shot back. "It's just that we don't believe it."

"There's nothing to believe," Vienna said. "We need to focus on your guest favors."

"You're right," Petal agreed and turned the pages in her catalogue. "None of these sound appealing," she flipped the book around to show Vienna and Carmy—who looked up from her phone. "Who wants a bar of expensive soap?"

"I would," Carmy said, laughing. "They sound like a lovely alternative to my dollar store shower gel, which I very much love, by the way."

"Sure you do," Petal said, shutting the catalogue. "I'm looking for something different. Something people would actually love and remember."

"Have you asked Romy?" Vienna asked, pulling the thread a bit. "She might have something in mind?"

"Yeah, and she told me to take care of this," Petal said. "She's dealing with other things."

Vienna noticed the sadness in her eyes. "Do you miss her?"

"Of course I miss her," Petal said, rolling her eyes. "But she'll be here in a couple weeks, so it's fine."

"Oh, this one is good," Carmy said, holding up her phone. "Customized M&Ms with you and Romy's faces printed on them."

"Carmy, that's not unique. No one even likes M&Ms."

"That's valid," Carmy said and went back to scrolling. "Everything is so generic these days. People can't even find different wedding destinations."

Petal looked at her, scrunching up her face. "Not my fault I wanted to have my wedding by the beach."

"Oh, it's not you. I meant someone else," Carmy said, motioning to Vienna with her eyes.

"You know I can hear and see you guys?"

"Yeah, with the way you're unravelling that couch by pulling that thread, we didn't realize you were actually mentally here."

"I'm sorry," Vienna said, letting go of the thread. "I'm just—" she shook her head and let it fall into her palms. "I'm fine. We should work on your guest favors."

Petal and Carmy looked at each other. Vienna knew what they were saying without words, but she really didn't want to bother them with the details.

"What have you guys come up with so far?"

"Absolutely nothing," Petal said. "I liked the idea Carmy gave of having cookies people can paint on, but that's going into their stomach later. I want something they can keep as a souvenir."

Suddenly, the word *souvenir* sparked an idea in Vienna.

"I don't know if you'll like this but..." she said, looking at Petal. "Earlier, at the market, I stopped by this beautiful bracelet shop where you get to choose the beads and charms to make one for yourself. The beads seemed different—maybe they're made here, I don't really know—but what about setting up something like that here so people can take home bracelets?"

"I love that," Carmy said excitedly. "This is so great, Vienna."

Petal didn't say anything for a couple of minutes. She just stood there looking at Vienna.

"You know what?" she finally said. "You're actually helpful these days."

Vienna laughed. "My pleasure."

"I'll check it out later today," Petal said. "Do either of you want to tag along?"

"I think I might," Carmy said, getting up. "I'm just going to take a bath. Call me when you leave."

Petal nodded while Carmy left the room. She went back to looking at the catalogues. "These things are outdated."

"But you seem to like them?"

"Unfortunately, some of them are entertaining."

"Did you know," Vienna asked, "that you'd end up like this?"

"Yes," she said. "I knew I'd spend my days looking at expensive guest favors in a catalogue I got off Amazon."

Vienna laughed. "Well, it suits you."

"I know."

Vienna leaned back into the couch, resisting the urge to start pulling at the thread again. "I think you just like being in control of everything."

Petal scoffed. "Obviously. If I don't, who will?"

Vienna smirked. "Romy?"

Petal let out a dramatic sigh. "She is the love of my life, but she's the least detail-oriented person I've ever met. If I left things up to her, we'd be handing out keychains from a gas station as guest favors."

Vienna laughed, nudging her knee against Petal's. "So, you like that she lets you take charge?"

Petal shrugged, flipping another page in the catalogue. "Yeah, I do. She balances me out. I stress; she calms me down. It works."

Vienna nodded, absorbing that. *Balancing out.* She wondered if she's ever had that—or whether she needed it. She thought about how there was once a point in her life where she thought everything was balanced out the way it was. Nothing really bothered her. Even now, nothing did. But something deep inside her felt like a void she'd avoided for so long. Maybe one day she'd find peace within herself and balance out that void she couldn't seem to point her finger at.

"Well," Petal said, letting out a long sigh. "Seems like there's one less thing to do on this long to-do list."

"Do you like my idea?"

"Yes," she said. "Unfortunately."

"You *love* it," Vienna teased. "Romy is going to love it too."

"She loves anything that I love, so it's a given."

"Well," Vienna said, "I'm going back to my room to sleep. I feel tired."

Petal nodded. "Are you happy for him?" she asked, taking Vienna by surprise.

"I don't know," she said. She took a moment. "I am."

Petal stared at her. Vienna knew that Petal wasn't really content with her answer—and she also knew that Petal knew she didn't really know what she was feeling.

What feeling could one have over the news of who was once their person getting married to someone completely new?

CHAPTER XVIII

Past

Carmy insisted on walking Vienna to her job at the pet store, even though Vienna said she could walk by herself.

"It's not like I *want* to accompany you," Carmy said. "I have something to do nearby."

Vienna nodded. "Fine by me," she said.

While walking, Vienna took out her black cap from her bag and put it on.

"How's your week been so far at the pet store?" Carmy asked.

Vienna groaned. "Don't ask me about it. The other day, a guy came in and asked if the hamster came with batteries. I said they're alive, and Carmy, believe me when I say he looked *very* disappointed."

Carmy gasped and then laughed. "Please don't tell me you gave that poor hamster to him."

"Obviously not. I told him to go to the toy store down the street," she said. "His reply was that he thought *this* was the toy store? The place is called *Pet-entially Yours,* for God's sake."

"Seems like you deal with a lot," Carmy said. "Do you like your job, though?"

"I don't really know," she said. "I'm just trying things out to see what works for me."

"You hated the cotton candy shop, so this might be even better."

"It's been a week," she said. "We'll see."

"This is me," she said when they reached the pet shop. "I'll catch you later."

Carmy waved back. She saw her continue walking through the glass doors from outside.

"You're finally here," her coworker—whose name she'd never cared to ask—said, putting his cap down. "I'm leaving. Make sure to close up," he added, forcing the keys into her hand. She nearly dropped them but caught them just in time.

She didn't really like her coworker, so she never spoke with him or got to know his name. Whenever she walked into the store during her shift, he always seemed to be eating a specific kind of burger and then leaving hurriedly. Today, he only seemed to be leaving hurriedly.

Vienna looked around. There were only two dogs and one cat, plenty of hamsters, rabbits, and a couple of rats too.

The place smelled like a rancid pack of potato chips at all times, which bothered her a lot and gave her mild migraines during her first week. She pulled out a jasmine-scented room spray from her bag, gave a few spritzes around the room, and sat by the counter.

There weren't really many customers most of the time. And even when they did come in, it was usually tiny children begging their parents to get a hamster. There was something about tiny rats that children really loved.

She poured some dog food for the dogs, fed the hamsters, and gave the rabbits a couple of carrots. There were a few new parrots that came in yesterday; they didn't really talk, so her shift was mostly silent.

Vienna grabbed the bowl of the cat, a grey Persian with a little white around the edges of his ears, which drooped most of the time. She opened a tin of cat food, poured it into his bowl, and placed it near his trunk. He stared at it for a couple of minutes, walked by it, smelled it, and went right back to his trunk.

Vienna scoffed. "You will die," she said to the cat. "This is your *third* day."

When she told her coworker the cat wasn't eating, he claimed the cat ate well during *his* shift. So, Vienna came to the conclusion that the cat just hated her.

"What even is your name exactly?" she said, going back to her seat. "Grumpaws?"

"I hope nobody heard that."

Vienna sighed. The cat meowed and seemed to get comfortable.

Vienna leaned back in the chair, watching as the cat stretched lazily on top of his trunk, completely ignoring the food she had just poured for him.

"You know," she said, rubbing her temples, "if you actually ate, I might start respecting you."

The cat let out a slow blink.

Vienna rolled her eyes and pulled out a magazine her coworker had left on the table. She flipped through it absentmindedly. There were a bunch of crosswords and word games that had already been completed.

A few minutes passed, the only sounds in the store being the occasional rustling from the rabbits and the faint chirping from the new parrots.

The peace was interrupted by the sharp jingle of the bell above the door. Vienna looked up to see a kid—probably around eight—dragging his tired-looking dad behind him.

"Hi," the boy said immediately, his eyes darting around the store like he was on a mission. "Do you guys sell snakes?"

Vienna stared at him. "No."

The kid frowned, clearly unimpressed by the answer. "Why not?"

"Because this is not a reptile store," she said, pointing toward the small mammals' section. "We do, however, have an excellent selection of rats."

The kid wrinkled his nose. "That's not the same thing."

"Well," Vienna said, "they both crawl."

The dad sighed, rubbing his eyes. "He's been talking about getting a pet snake for weeks."

"Then you might want to try the exotic pet store on the next street over," Vienna offered. "This place is less exotic."

The dad snorted at that but quickly covered it with a cough. "Alright, buddy. No snakes today. Let's go."

The kid groaned dramatically but didn't fight it. Before leaving, though, he stared at the Persian cat still lounging on the trunk.

"What's wrong with him?" he asked, pointing.

Vienna glanced at the cat, who was still stubbornly ignoring his food.

"I don't know," she said.

The kid nodded in understanding. "I think he's being dramatic, like my brother."

Vienna smirked as the boy and his dad walked out. As soon as the door shut behind them, she turned back to the cat.

"See? Even eight-year-olds know you're being difficult."

The cat flicked his tail in her direction but still refused to eat.

Vienna sighed, shaking her head. "Fine. Starve."

But later, when she passed by his trunk again, she noticed the bowl was empty.

She smiled. She knew he'd come around

CHAPTER XIX

Present

Vienna woke up feeling wary. She didn't want to get out of bed. The only time she did was to shut the curtains—the sun was bothering her.

She ignored Petal's calls and Carmy's constant knocking, telling her to come out. She told them to go away, claiming she was sick and it'd be dangerous for them to come in since they might catch it too. She knew Carmy didn't believe her, but she left her alone.

Being in a constant state where she didn't know why she felt the way she did, she was sometimes hit by waves of sadness she couldn't explain. She didn't know what to do other than lie on her bed and stare up at the ceiling. It looked weirdly poetic—almost like a painting, with wildflower drawings and grapevines.

Vienna stayed in bed, staring at the ceiling.

The patterns on the hotel ceiling weren't like the ones at home. No familiar wildflowers or vines, just an off-white surface with tiny imperfections in the paint. She tried to find shapes in them, like how people did with clouds, but all she could see were uneven brushstrokes and a grey stain near the corner.

She turned over, pressing her face into the pillow. The sheets smelled like detergent—too clean, too unfamiliar. The air conditioner hummed softly in the background, the only real sound in the room.

It was quiet.

Too quiet.

She had told Petal and Carmy she wasn't feeling well, which wasn't exactly a lie. She just wasn't sick in the way they thought. She needed a day where nothing happened—no wedding talk, no forced conversations, no pretending she wasn't carrying something heavy she didn't know how to put down.

She'd heard shuffling a couple hours earlier while half-asleep, but didn't check it out. She already knew who it'd be. The only sign either Petal or Carmy had been there was the small paper bag sitting outside her door.

Vienna eyed it from the bed. She already knew what was inside—coffee, maybe a muffin. A peace offering. A quiet reminder that they were still thinking about her, even when she shut them out.

She *should* open the door and take it. She *should* send them a message, let them know she was fine.

Instead, she pulled the blanket over her head and closed her eyes.

She must have fallen asleep at some point, because the next thing she knew, the light in the room had shifted. The sun had lowered, casting long golden streaks across the floor.

Vienna sat up, groggy, her throat dry. She rubbed her eyes and turned toward the door again.

The bag was still there.

She sighed, finally pushing off the blankets and walking over to grab it.

Coffee. And, of course, a muffin.

She set the cup down on the desk near the window, peeling back the lid slightly. It was cold, but she didn't mind—she didn't feel like drinking water to quench her thirst.

She hesitated, then sat down, pulling her legs up onto the chair. She took a sip. It wasn't exactly how she liked it, but it wasn't bad either.

She picked apart the muffin, not really eating it.

She had no idea how long she'd been sitting like this—picking it apart and sipping the cold coffee. The room was dim now, the last bit of daylight slipping through the heavy curtains. She thought about turning on the lamp but didn't. Darkness felt easier.

The air conditioner clicked off, leaving the room eerily silent.

Vienna stared at the window, at the faint outline of the ocean beyond the glass. From here, it looked still, motionless, like it wasn't moving at all. But she knew better. It never really stopped—waves pulling back just to crash forward again.

She didn't know why that thought sat so heavy in her chest.

Somewhere outside, laughter echoed down the hall. Someone knocked on a distant door. A muffled voice answered. Life happening just outside this room.

Vienna set the coffee down and rubbed at her temples. She wasn't sad. At least, she didn't *think* she was. She just felt... off. Like there was something sitting at the edge of her mind that she didn't want to look at too closely.

Maybe tomorrow, she'd feel normal again.

Maybe she wouldn't.

But either way, the night would pass. The sun would rise. The ocean would keep moving.

She still wasn't hungry, but she finally took a bite of the muffin anyway.

It wasn't as bad as she expected it to be.

CHAPTER XX

Past

Going up the hill wasn't really Vienna's forte, but she agreed to do it when Eden convinced her—and brought her friends too. Carmy and Petal were weirdly energetic about the whole thing, and she didn't really get it.

Eden kept checking in on her whenever she lagged a few feet behind and tried to match her pace, which was almost always. She wasn't tired, but she wasn't excited either.

"The view will be so worth it," Carmy said, rubbing Vienna's arm lightly with a smile. "Trust me."

Vienna nodded and continued walking. There were a few other people on the hike too, but none of them looked like they didn't want to be there. They seemed tired, sure—but that was it.

Petal was leading the way. Vienna knew she was energetic because she'd done sports all her life. This hike came to her so effortlessly it was almost like breathing—she wasn't even puffing like Vienna or Carmy, whose cheeks were flushed red.

Eden was just being himself: walking quietly, not interrupting the conversations between her and Carmy, but still listening and nodding along when needed.

Vienna knew this hike had been his plan to get her out of the house. That's why he made sure to invite both Petal and Carmy—it had been his idea.

The only thing she liked about the hike so far was looking at the different types of rocks and pebbles. They fascinated her. Some were green and looked like glass, but they were just a type of rock.

She was thrilled to find one and slip it into her pocket. "They're so cute."

Eden smiled. "They are. I'll help you find more."

Vienna nodded. "I'd like to find these pebbles without having to walk."

"That's not how this works," Eden said, walking past her. "Where's the thrill in that?"

Vienna shook her head and followed him.

They reached the top of the hill just as the sun began to set. She realized maybe the effort had been worth it—because from that point, she and the sun were both looking over her city. The orange light lit up the buildings, which looked minuscule from up there. Suddenly, life didn't seem that complicated. Everything looked tiny but shiny from that height. She felt lighter.

Petal sat down on the dry hilltop, brushing the sand from her hands. "This is so beautiful. I feel awesome."

Carmy laughed. "Don't you do this like every other month?"

"Hell yeah," Petal said. "Look at this beauty."

"I agree," Eden said, taking off his cap. "You get in some exercise, a beautiful view—and even some delicious food."

"You did not," Vienna laughed.

"Yes, I did," Eden said, pulling out a brown paper bag. She recognized that shade of brown instantly—it was burgers from the place down the street from Eden's apartment. She didn't usually indulge in junk food, but she loved *those* burgers, and made sure to have one every time she visited him.

"I got food for everyone," Eden said.

"Oh, thank god," Petal groaned. "I really didn't want to eat Carmy's sushi."

Carmy rolled her eyes. "I wouldn't have packed it if Eden had *mentioned* he was bringing food."

"Sorry," he said. "I wanted it to be a surprise for Vivi. But we *are* eating your sushi too—at least, I am. I'm starving."

Vienna grabbed the bag from him and sat down next to Petal. She opened it up and handed out a burger to everyone, then pulled out the giant bag of fries and placed it at the center of their circle.

As soon as she bit into the burger, the hike finally seemed worth it. Overlooking the sky, now dark with lingering hues of orange and red, she watched as city lights slowly replaced the fading sun.

"The walk back down is going to be scary," Carmy said, leaning in for a fry.

"It's okay," Vienna replied. "You have us."

"This is some good fucking burger," Petal said, mouth full.

"I know, right?" Vienna almost shouted. "We've lived in this city our whole lives, but how come we've never found this place?"

"I have no clue."

"They should replace wedding food with these burgers, honestly," Petal said. "Wedding food is outrageous. The other day, I had beans on some mush—I don't even know what that was."

"I think weddings are a lot of work," Carmy said. "But very beautiful. I adore them."

"I agree," Eden said. "Something about two people deciding to be together for the rest of their lives is wonderful."

"People divorce all the time," Vienna said, taking another bite. "I don't think marriage means anything."

"That's on them," Petal said. "But I think people should do whatever they like—get married, get divorced, get drunk, become a heroin addict, who cares."

Everyone laughed. It was true. People had free will. They could do anything they wanted. But Vienna still didn't like the idea of throwing a whole ceremony just to prove she loved someone.

"I want to get married," Carmy said. "I think I'd like that."

"Yeah, me too," Eden agreed. "I see my parents—they're still happy and in love. I want that."

"I don't think I want to be married," Petal said. "But I also want to get married? I don't really know. I haven't thought about it."

"I don't think I'll ever be married," Vienna added.

"Why is that?" Eden asked.

"That just isn't me," Vienna replied. "It doesn't sound like something I'd like to be in."

Carmy nodded. "Well, we're just nineteen," she said. "We have time to figure everything out."

Everyone agreed—they were young, and there was so much time ahead.

The rest of the night was filled with talk about university and what they wanted to do next. The thing was, no one really knew. They were content with where they stood and knew they'd deal with things when the time came—but they also knew how time catches up.

On the way down the hill, Vienna kept looking for the glowing pebbles. Every time she thought she found a shiny one, it turned out to be just a piece of broken glass. She hoped to find one more—because she knew she wasn't going to be climbing up another hill anytime soon, and she wanted something to remember it by.

Disappointed, she got into the car after waving goodbye to Carmy and Petal. She went nonverbal the entire ride home—not because she was sad, but because she was tired and just wanted to sleep.

When they finally reached her house and she was about to get out of the car, Eden touched her arm, stopping her. She looked at him and noticed he was reaching into the pocket of his black hoodie.

He reached for her hand—and something cold touched her palm.

She looked down as he pulled his hand back.

It was a shiny pink pebble.

CHAPTER XXI

Present

Petal was scrolling on her phone impatiently. Carmy and Vienna shared a look.

"You know," Carmy started, "we came to eat here so you could take some time off to cool down."

"Sorry, Romy's coming in two days," Petal said, putting her phone down. "There's a lot to do."

"That's why you have us. You can take a breather."

Petal nodded. Vienna gave her a tired smile.

She'd made herself leave her room after Carmy suggested breakfast at a nearby café. At first, she was hesitant, but then she finally opened her door, startling Carmy.

"I'm coming too," she'd said.

The café was mostly normal for the area—one of those Parisian-inspired places where people preferred sitting outside. But the sun was scorching, and even the blue patio umbrella above them couldn't shield them completely. Sitting outside wasn't a great idea.

Vienna stirred her cappuccino. She didn't know why she'd ordered something hot in this heat instead of a cold drink, but she'd gone with it.

The bowl of queso sat in the middle, staring at her. She wasn't really hungry, but it looked appealing enough.

She dunked a piece of bread into the queso, letting the cheese drip slightly before taking a small bite. It was good. Warm, salty, with just enough spice. She chewed slowly as Carmy and Petal debated something about wedding décor.

The café buzzed with background noise—plates clinking, silverware scraping against ceramic, the faint hum of conversation. Outside, the sunlight reflected off patio tables, making the air feel even hotter.

Vienna leaned back in her chair, hoping for a breeze, and took another sip of her cappuccino.

Then, from somewhere behind her, she heard a voice. A familiar one.

"Wait... is that you, Vienna?"

She turned her head slightly, squinting up at the figure standing near their table.

A man—early or maybe late twenties. Tall, slightly disheveled brown hair, aviator sunglasses resting on top of his head. He held a smoothie in one hand and a to-go bag in the other, a slight look of amusement crossing his face.

Vienna stared.

She knew him. She just didn't know *from where*.

There was something vaguely familiar about his voice, the way he stood, the way he looked at her like he already knew her—but was waiting for her to place him.

"Wow," he said, shifting the bag to his other hand. "Didn't think I'd run into *you* here."

Vienna blinked.

Carmy and Petal had both gone quiet, watching with thinly veiled curiosity.

She could feel the weight of the moment pressing against her. She was supposed to say something, to recognize him. She didn't. Not fully.

So, she went with the safest option.

"Hey," she said, keeping her tone light but noncommittal.

The man raised an eyebrow, waiting for her to follow up with something else.

She didn't.

After a beat, he smirked, sipping from his smoothie.

"You don't remember me, do you?"

Vienna exhaled through her nose and shook her head. "Not really."

Petal shot Carmy a look, probably wondering if they should jump in. Neither did.

"Damn," the guy said, clearly more amused than offended. "Makes sense. We didn't actually talk that much."

That didn't help either.

Vienna tilted her head. "Then remind me."

He grinned, setting the to-go bag down beside them like he had all the time in the world.

"Eden's birthday party," he said. "The one at his apartment, two years ago? You were there."

Her stomach tightened slightly.

She remembered the party. Not all of it, but enough. Mostly because she left earlier than intended. She'd barely spoken to anyone except Eden. Everyone in that room had seemed to live in a world she didn't feel a part of.

She stared at the guy again, narrowing her eyes as she searched her memory.

And then—something clicked.

Not a full memory, just a flash.

Him, sitting across from her at Eden's kitchen table, talking to someone else about a new job he was considering.

Vienna had barely paid attention, tracing circles along the rim of her wine glass while Eden laughed too loudly at something across the room.

She still didn't know his name. But she did remember *one* thing.

"You're the guy who was going on and on about moving to London," she said slowly. "You never shut up about it."

Petal let out a choked laugh, covering her mouth with her hand.

Vienna looked at her, confused. She hadn't meant it as a joke—that was simply what she remembered.

The guy pressed a hand to his chest, mock offense on his face. "That's what you remember?"

Vienna shrugged. "It's all you talked about."

He laughed, shaking his head. "Fair. I did end up moving there, though. For about a year."

Vienna nodded, unsure what else to say.

Carmy leaned in slightly. "And you are...?"

"Oh," he said, extending a hand toward her. "Wade."

Carmy shook his hand. Then Petal did the same.

Vienna didn't move.

Wade seemed to catch the shift almost immediately. His gaze flickered back toward her, debating whether or not to say something.

He did anyway.

"So," he said—casual, but deliberate—"are you guys here for Eden's wedding? I didn't know you were still in touch with him."

Carmy went stiff beside her. Petal sipped her drink a little too quickly.

Vienna tilted her head, her expression unreadable. "Not really."

Wade raised an eyebrow. "Not really?"

Her grip tightened around her coffee cup.

"Here for Petal's wedding, not his," she said finally.

Wade let out a small hum of acknowledgment and nodded. "Huh. Anyways, congrats, Petal."

Vienna glanced sideways as Petal nodded and muttered a thank-you.

No one said much after that. Carmy and Petal didn't jump in, probably hoping Vienna would.

Wade didn't seem to mind the silence. He looked like he'd already gotten what he needed from her reaction.

"Well," he said, stepping back and grabbing his to-go bag, "it was good running into you. I'll let Eden know you're here—he'll be thrilled."

Vienna forced a small smile that didn't reach her eyes. "Sure."

Wade gave a lazy salute before disappearing into the crowd.

Vienna sat back in her chair, exhaling slowly.

Carmy nudged her lightly. "That was... something."

Vienna huffed a laugh. It wasn't real—just something to ease the tension around the table. "That was annoying."

Petal set down her cup, watching her carefully. "You okay?"

Vienna wasn't sure what she was.

It wasn't sadness. It wasn't anger.

Just... *something*.

She took another bite of queso-covered bread, chewing slowly before answering.

"I'm fine."

But she wasn't really fine with running into people from a chapter she thought was closed—especially not in an island miles beyond her.

CHAPTER XXII

Past

The pet shop was silent as usual. Even the parrots had been sold out a couple of days ago, so there were no sounds from them either—just the slight bell sound from the door whenever a breeze passed by, which was rare.

The dogs were sleeping, which was what they always did. The cat she had come to adore was also sleeping, so she was left alone to sit with her thoughts and her coworker's unfinished crossword book.

She flipped through it, mentally completing each crossword. They weren't as hard as she thought they'd be. She reminded herself to bring books to read, which she completely kept forgetting about.

As she turned to the next page, the bell rang, notifying her that someone had walked in. She looked up to assist. It was a boy around ten years old with a much older lady—most likely his mom.

"Do you guys have any cats we can take home?"

It felt like a pang to her chest. She wanted to say they didn't have any, but she knew she couldn't do that—and she couldn't keep him locked up here anyway.

"Yes, we do," she said. "One grey Persian cat."
But the boy ran toward his crate before she finished speaking.

"Mom, he is fat," he said, pointing to the cat.

Vienna just stared at him. She wished she could say, *You can't take him*, but she didn't know what stopped her either.

"Oh, thank you," the woman said, walking toward the boy. "He's been asking me for a cat for a week. I just want to get this over with."

And just like that, her only companion was gone. She didn't really look at the cat when she explained to the mother how to feed him, his vaccination routines, and the answers to her other questions.

For the next couple of days, Vienna's shifts were excruciatingly painful.

She convinced herself it wasn't the cat.

It had been three days since the cat left.

Vienna told herself it didn't matter.

It was just a cat.

But the shop felt emptier without him.

She still found herself glancing at his old spot out of habit, expecting to see him stretched lazily across the crate. She had even almost poured food into his empty bowl yesterday before realizing he wasn't there.

She told herself it didn't matter.

And then, the bell rang.

She looked up from the counter, immediately recognizing the boy and his mother from earlier.

Vienna's eyes flickered down to the carrier in the woman's hands. The grey Persian cat stared back at her through the bars.

Something in her chest twisted.

The boy looked far less enthusiastic than he had a few days ago. His mother sighed, setting the carrier down on the counter.

"He won't eat," she said. "We tried everything. He just sits in the corner all day. Doesn't move. Doesn't drink. Nothing."

Vienna swallowed. "Maybe he's just adjusting. It can take some time."

The woman shook her head. "It's been three days. My son wanted a playful cat, and he just... doesn't do anything."

The boy crossed his arms. "I wanted a fun cat."

Vienna gritted her teeth. She knew she couldn't say what she really wanted to.

Instead, she exhaled slowly, glancing at the cat.

He looked the same as always—half-lidded eyes, expression unreadable. But there was something a little off. Maybe it was how his ears were drooped lower than usual. Or how his paws were tucked too tightly beneath him, like he was trying to make himself small.

Vienna hated how much she understood that feeling.

She looked back at the mother, already knowing what was coming next.

"We'd like to return him," the woman said, placing the adoption papers on the counter.

Vienna shouldn't have felt relieved—but she did.

She bent down, unlocking the crate without thinking.

The cat blinked up at her, unmoving at first. Then, slowly—so slowly—he stepped forward, brushing against her wrist.

The warmth of his fur sent something sharp through her chest.

Vienna swallowed.

"I'll take him."

The words slipped out before she even processed them.

The mother blinked. "What?"

"I'll take him," Vienna repeated, standing up straight. "You don't have to return him. I'll take him home."

The woman looked relieved. The boy just shrugged. "Okay."

The handover was quick, impersonal. A few signatures, a brief exchange of words, and just like that—he was hers.

She picked him up, holding him against her chest.
For the first time since she met him, he purred.
Vienna smiled softly, running a hand over his fur.
"Lucky," she murmured.
She wasn't sure if she meant him or herself.

CHAPTER XXIII

Present

Vienna was getting ready to go help out Petal at her wedding venue. She was stuck between wanting to wear the floral skirt or plain jeans to pair with her lilac top. She felt like her naturally red hair didn't fit pastel tones very well, but Carmy said otherwise—so she went with it.

She brushed her hair and put on perfume that she didn't really remember where she got from. It smelled like strawberries and something else she couldn't quite place. She didn't particularly like strawberries, so she had no idea why she'd gotten it.

Just as she was about to open the door, there were a couple of knocks.

"There's mail for Vienna Vittori," a deep but gruff voice said from behind the door.

She pulled it open to be met with a man, much older than her—maybe in his late fifties—in a navy-blue suit. He held out the mail.

Vienna muttered a "thank you" while receiving it.

"Have a good day," the man said and left.

She was confused as she examined the thick white envelope. She opened it and pulled out a white card.

In bold, cursive, gold-plated letters, it read:

Eden Nightstone Marries Nalia Fabien

Followed by a bunch of details she did not care about. She was more worried about how Eden knew what hotel she was staying at—because she didn't remember telling that to him or Nalia, for that matter. But she wasn't surprised. Word gets around, and it wasn't like there were a bunch of hotels to stay at on this island.

Still, it bothered her a little. But she was aware that the fact she was holding her ex's wedding invitation in her hands *should* bother her more.

Vienna placed the invitation on the table by the door and left the room. As she placed her room's keycard on the sensor, a very paranoid Carmy walked toward her in a hurry.

"Whoa," Vienna said, throwing her hands up. "Don't walk too fast, you're literally scaring the tiny human growing inside you."

"Did you get it?" Carmy asked, her eyes wide.

"Get what?"

"Eden's invitation?"

"Yes? You walked that fast to ask me that?"

Carmy nodded, her cheeks now visibly flushed and red. "I am going to kill him."

Vienna laughed and started walking. "It's not that big of a deal," she said. "Did he send you one too?"

"Yes. And to Petal too," Carmy replied. "I can't believe he'd send you one. Is he stupid?"

"That's just good old Eden," she said. "He can't hate anyone."

"You didn't do anything worthy of hating," Carmy said, but quietly.

"Maybe," Vienna said—but she didn't really mean it. She knew what she did, and she was okay putting up with that. "That's up to him."

As she walked down the stairs, she didn't know what to think of the invitation, really. It wasn't like she was going to go. That was never in the plan. This was all becoming too tiring for her. She didn't want to run into Eden halfway across the world just to find out he was getting married.

It wasn't the *marrying* part that bothered her. She worried that her friends might have to walk on eggshells around her when they were here for *Petal's* special day.

She saw Petal waiting by the hotel's entrance, and Petal extended her arms as soon as she laid eyes on Vienna, pulling her into a hug. She awkwardly hugged her back. They weren't really huggers—Carmy was, but she and Petal weren't—so Vienna knew Petal was worried about her.

"I'm fine," she said. "Really."

"I can't believe he'd do this," Petal said, pulling her shades down from her head and adjusting her red tote bag. "What was he even thinking?"

"I know, right?" Carmy shot back. "It's like he wants to rub it in Vie's face all over."

Vienna really didn't want to be the topic of conversation right now, so she started walking.

"I think we should get going."

They followed her while still bickering about Eden. Even though she mentioned multiple times that he probably did it with good intentions, they refused to agree.

"You don't send your wedding invitation to your ex no matter what terms you *think* you're on," said Carmy.

"I don't think he did it to rub it all over my face," Vienna said, mocking. "I don't care what intentions he had—it doesn't matter. Because I'm not going."

"You definitely shouldn't," Carmy said. "I wouldn't."

"Yeah, you guys have *my* wedding to attend and then get the fuck out of here," Petal said. "I can't believe he wants to have his wedding here, out of all the places in the world."

"You can't think that way," Vienna said, concerned. "He doesn't exist to us."

All she wanted was for Petal to not worry about her problems. She already had a lot on her plate, and Eden shouldn't be one of them.

The scooters that went past them were stirring up a lot of dust, and they had to cover their mouths while speaking.

"Carmy, did you bring a mask?" asked Vienna.

"Nope," she replied. "I do have a scarf, so I can use that?"

"Please do," Petal said. "I'm starting to worry about you. Are you sure you shouldn't be seeing a doctor?"

"I'm fine," she said. "The other day, I video-called my doctor—everything's fine."

"Doctors are video-calling these days?"

"Yep," Carmy said, putting the scarf around her mouth. "Mine does."

"That's good," Vienna said, adjusting her top.

As they reached Petal's wedding venue, the one thing on Vienna's mind was how to avoid the topic of Eden altogether so they could focus on Petal's wedding. But she wondered if she was really okay with everything that was going on—and the unknown weight in her chest that was tiring her out, even if everything on the outside seemed fine.

CHAPTER XXIV

Past

The waffle café smelled like warm vanilla, melting chocolate, and caramelized sugar—the kind of place that felt cozy but not too crowded, loud but not overwhelming.

Vienna sat across from Eden at a small corner table, watching as he drizzled an unnecessary amount of syrup over his waffles.

"You're going to regret that," she said, taking a sip of her milkshake.

Eden grinned, completely unfazed. "Regret is for people who don't live in the moment."

Vienna rolled her eyes but didn't argue.

She'd ordered something simple—a scoop of vanilla ice cream with kiwis. Nothing drowning in syrup or overflowing with toppings. Eden, on the other hand, had gone all out with a stack of golden waffles, whipped cream, Nutella, and enough syrup to flood the plate.

"You're just jealous," he added, taking a ridiculous bite.

Vienna smirked. "Of what, a sugar coma?"

Eden pointed at her with his fork. "Of the fact that I'm embracing happiness, and you're sitting there eating something that looks like it came straight out of a diet plan."

Vienna huffed, stabbing a strawberry with her fork. "I like what I like."

"Yeah, yeah," Eden said through a mouthful of waffle. "Remind me to introduce you to the concept of indulgence later."

Vienna just shook her head, letting the conversation settle into comfortable silence. The café buzzed around them—the clinking of spoons, the faint hum of coffee machines, bursts of laughter from nearby tables.

She liked it here.

The simplicity of it. The warmth of the place. The way her ice cream was customizable. The way Eden always managed to get chocolate somewhere on his face without realizing it.

It was nice.

Before she could complete her thought, she was cut off by a loud voice.

"Holy shit, no way!"

Vienna barely had time to look up before a guy clapped Eden on the back, grinning.

Eden laughed, setting his fork down as he turned toward the voice. "Dude! What are you doing here?"

Vienna blinked, registering the presence of a stranger before she could even react.

The guy was tall, casually dressed in a hoodie and jeans, a little scruffy but effortlessly put together. There was something easy about the way he carried himself—like he was always at home wherever he went.

Vienna had seen him before.

Not often, but enough to recognize his face.

One of Eden's friends from somewhere.

Not someone she had ever really spoken to.

"I just got back in town last week," the guy said, sliding into the seat next to Eden without hesitation. "Figured I'd get some food, but man, I didn't expect to run into you."

Eden grinned. "How long are you here?"

"A while, actually. Thinking about sticking around," the guy said, reaching for a menu from the holder on the table.

He didn't even glance at Vienna.

She sat back slightly, resting her elbow on the table.

She wasn't offended. Not really. This wasn't the first time something like this had happened.

Eden had a way of falling into conversations that didn't leave much room for anyone else.

It wasn't intentional. It wasn't malicious.

It was just how things always played out.

She watched as they talked—laughing, exchanging stories about people she didn't know, places she'd never been.

She could have jumped in. Said something. Made herself known.

But what was there to say?

She took another bite of her ice cream instead, slowly chewing on the kiwi. She focused on the water droplet sliding down the outside of her ice cream cup.

The spoon clinked against the glass, but neither of them looked at her.

She let her gaze drift toward the window. The café door opened and closed. People came and went.

The air smelled like melted ice cream and fresh waffles. A couple sat near the counter, splitting a sundae, their spoons clicking against each other as they reached into the same bowl.

Vienna tapped her fingers lightly against the table, zoning in and out of the conversation happening right in front of her.

She wasn't mad.

She wasn't even annoyed.

It was just one of those things.

Eventually, the guy stood up, still holding his menu. "Alright, man, I'll let you eat, but we gotta catch up properly. Let's grab a drink later this week."

Eden nodded. "For sure. Hit me up."

They fist-bumped, exchanged a few more words, and then he walked off to the counter.

Vienna waited.

Eden turned back to his waffles like nothing had happened.

He didn't notice the shift in her posture—the way her shoulders had tensed slightly, the way she was playing with her spoon instead of eating.

It took a full thirty seconds before he glanced up at her, finally registering her silence.

"What?" he asked.

Vienna just shook her head, stirring the melting ice cream in her bowl. "Nothing."

Eden raised an eyebrow, still chewing. "You sure?"

"Yeah," she said, popping another kiwi into her mouth. "Just thinking."

Eden didn't push. He went back to his food, and Vienna let the conversation drift into something else.

She wasn't going to bring it up.

Not this.

Not something that small.

She told herself it didn't matter.

Because maybe it didn't.

Or maybe it was just easier to pretend it didn't.

"So, how's your cat Lucky?"

Vienna dug into her ice cream, not really scooping it up. "He's great, you should come see him."

"I am so jealous of him," he said. "He gets to live with you. He is lucky indeed."

Vienna looked up and smiled. It didn't really reach her eyes.

"Except he is eating through everything. I'm not sure if I'll even be able to feed myself later."

Eden laughed. Vienna laughed along with him—but deep down, her heart tugged at the edges, hoping she would cry it out or worse, scream at him.

But she knew she'd do neither.

CHAPTER XXV

Present

Vienna was in her best dress in a while—she had to be, because Petal had specifically picked it out for her bachelorette party, and she loved it. Her hair was tied in a high ponytail, and the grey plaid halter-neck dress with white accents and small ribbons at the front made her feel like herself again, for the first time in a long time.

Carmy tightened the ponytail a little more, making Vienna wince.

"Sorry," Carmy muttered.

"It's fine." Vienna smiled at Carmy's reflection in the mirror. "You look beautiful."

Carmy wore a grey dress similar to hers, but instead of a halter neck, it had a high neckline that suited her perfectly. Her dark brown hair was styled half up, half down, framing her radiant face.

"So do you," she replied.

"We should get going to Petal's room," Vienna said, and the two of them left together.

They knocked on Petal's door, which was opened by Romy, still in her bathrobe.

"Oh, girls," Romy said, stepping aside. "Both of you look lovely. Petal's still getting ready."

Romy had piercing blue eyes that sometimes-unsettled Vienna. Romy was a wonderful person, but those eyes had a way of unnerving her. She noticed Romy now had bangs falling just in front of them.

"Nice hair," Vienna said. "The bangs suit you."

"Oh, thank you," Romy replied.

"Where are you going?" Carmy asked, pushing aside the hair curler on the bed before sitting down.

"I'm having a little get-together with my friends too," Romy said. "Nothing as crazy as you guys, though."

"You should join us," Vienna offered. "I mean, it's just us three on the boat."

"No, this is Petal's Day. She should have her bachelorette however she wants. I'm not a party person."

Which was true. In all the time Vienna had known Romy, she'd never seen her go clubbing or out much at all. Not because she disliked it, but because she seemed content staying in—very unlike Vienna, who didn't love staying in or going out.

Petal came out of the bathroom, looking stunning in a long, silky grey dress.

"Oh wow," Romy said. "Do a twirl for us."

Petal laughed and twirled awkwardly. "Is this enough?"

"Yes," Romy smiled. "You go have fun."

Vienna wasn't sure how she felt about boats. As soon as they began sailing away from the island, nausea hit her. Petal opened a bottle of champagne while Carmy shouted, "To being a bride!"

Vienna cheered, forcing the sickness down. Petal poured champagne for herself and into Vienna's flute, then grabbed a bottle of apple juice from the nearby table and filled Carmy's.

They all clinked glasses and started drinking.

As the night went on, Vienna began to settle in. The nausea had passed—maybe because of the food, but probably the three more flutes of champagne that followed.

"I can't believe you're getting married in a couple days," Carmy said, hugging Petal sideways. "I'm so happy for you."

"Thank you," Petal said, downing her drink.

"We used to sit like this in our rooms," Vienna said. "Now we're far from our rooms, drinking in the middle of the ocean."

"We've grown a lot," Petal said, looking down. The sound of waves crashing was more noticeable now, and the air had turned chillier.

"I didn't think we'd grow up so fast," Carmy said, slowly shaking her head and zoning out. "I can't believe it."

"You guys have," Vienna said, laughing while finishing her drink. "You've done way more at twenty-four than I have."

"You're successful too. You literally bought the pet shop you used to work part-time at. That's something."

Vienna smiled and nodded. "You guys are doing real adult things."

Petal and Carmy exchanged a glance—an understanding look that, for the first time in their nearly ten-year friendship, Vienna couldn't quite decipher. Maybe it meant they had each other to navigate this terrifying life. Maybe it meant *we've made it*. Whatever it was, Vienna was happy they had each other.

The sailboat stopped somewhere in the open water. Vienna wasn't sure where exactly, but the full, bright moon was clearly visible. A sudden wave of sadness crashed into her. Maybe this was one of the last times they'd all be together like this.

In three months, Carmy would become a mother. Petal would be moving after the wedding. And all of it was hitting Vienna at once.

"This is probably the last time I'll see you guys like this," she said, eyes brimming with tears that refused to fall. "In a couple months, you'll both be in different places, doing life."

Carmy was already crying, wiping her cheeks. Petal just looked out at the sea.

"I shouldn't have said anything," Vienna muttered. "I'm such a downer," she laughed.

"You're right," Carmy said, sniffing. "I'm going to miss you guys." She wiped another tear. "I'm sorry—it's the pregnancy hormones."

Petal turned around and hugged her. Vienna joined in.

"We'll always have each other," Petal said, her voice muffled in the embrace. "We can do this anytime. Just one call away."

"I haven't been away from you guys since I was fourteen. I don't know how to do life without you both."

"Do you remember how we used to play that game in my garden?" Petal asked.

Vienna nodded. "*To-bes and maybes*?"

"It was so funny," Petal said, laughing at the memory. "Why did we bring a bunch of deck cards and dice, hoping the numbers we added up would match?"

"It wasn't dumb," Vienna said. "Even though we almost never got the numbers I wanted."

"But it was *our* game," she added.

"It was," Carmy agreed. "You know the thing about games of probability? One thing stays constant."

"Which is?" Petal asked.

"Us," Carmy said. "The players. No matter what number we got—win or lose—we stayed and kept the game going."

Vienna was trying not to break down. "But you guys won't be there to play with me," she said, voice cracking. "How can I go on?"

"As you always have," Petal said, grabbing her hand tightly. "Just... without us."

"I'm not going anywhere," Carmy shot back. "Just without *Petal*."

Vienna laughed. They all did.

Life had crept up on them quietly, just like the rest of the night. But it only felt like home because they were in each other's lives, shaping it as one.

CHAPTER XXVI

Past

Vienna lay on her bed, cuddling her cat, Lucky. It had been about three months since she brought him home, and in that time, she had figured out what he liked and didn't. One of his favorite things was lying on top of her stomach while she read a book in bed.

Eden lay near her feet, gently caressing her calf. The bed was cramped—meant for just one person—but there they were, spread out together, while the warm, dry summer air blew through the open window, making her pink curtains flutter.

"Are you comfortable?" Vienna asked, pulling her book down. "Aren't you too big?"

"Lucky is big," Eden said playfully. "He should get down."

Vienna laughed. "He won't, you know that."

Eden reached out and poked Lucky, who lazily looked up and went back to napping. "Wow, he hates me."

"He hates everyone," she said. "Including me."

"He doesn't hate *you*. You seem like the only person he loves."

Vienna shrugged. Lately, she hadn't been hanging out with Eden as much. She was busy with college work and the pet shop, but even when she was free, she couldn't bring herself to spend time with him like before. Ever since that conversation at the ice cream shop, something had been bothering her. It had been a while now, and she couldn't exactly bring it up again—so she let it go. But even then, something still felt off, though she couldn't pinpoint what.

"You know," he said, sitting up, "there's an event happening at my college. You should come."

"When is it?"

"This Friday evening?"

She shut her book and placed it on the table beside her bed. "I can't really come—I've got a shift at the store."

"Oh yeah, I forgot about that," he said. "Well, if you can, try to."

Vienna nodded. "But what's the point?" she said. "It's not like your friends particularly like me."

"What?" he said. "They do. It just takes them time to settle in."

"It's been a year."

But it wasn't just that—it was the way she didn't even know any of their names. They never introduced themselves unless Eden did, and they often talked over her like she wasn't even there. The worst part was, Eden had never acknowledged it.

At first, it had bothered her quietly. But now, after knowing him and his friends for a year, she wasn't really sure they even *wanted* her there. She didn't know if *he* wanted her there either. It was starting to feel like pity invites—but she could never say that to him. She knew how he'd take it. And maybe it wasn't a big deal anyway. She could deal with it.

"Well," he said, "they can be like that. But that doesn't mean they don't like you."

"Yeah." Vienna gave a weak smile. "But I have work anyway, so I'll try."

Eden nodded. "Do you want any food?"

"I'm not hungry," Vienna said, getting off the bed. "But you can order in, if you want."

Eden rubbed the back of his neck. His index finger had a single silver band on it. He always wore it—he never took it off, as far as she'd seen.

"I've been meaning to ask," Vienna said, dragging her comforter. "What does that ring mean?"

He brought his hand forward. "This?" he pointed.

Vienna nodded, folding the comforter. "You never take it off."

"Yeah. A friend gave it to me in seventh grade," he said, twisting it around. "It just stuck with me, I guess."

"Are you still in touch with them?"

"Yeah," he said. "He moved for college—about five hours away. I even visited him last year, remember?"

She nodded again. She didn't remember, but she didn't want to get into the details. There *was* a time last year when he went away for about a week, but she wasn't sure if that was the friend he was referring to.

The thought settled deep into her mind: Eden knew her friends. They even hung out sometimes. But she didn't know *any* of his. That was weird. Still, she kept brushing it off like it was nothing—because maybe it *was* nothing.

She placed the folded comforter beside Eden and ruffled her pillows. "I'm going to make some coffee. Do you want some?"

"Nope," he said, tugging at her shirt absentmindedly. "I'm going to order in. You sure you don't want anything?"

"Yes, I'm sure."

"You can't just live off coffee and flavored yogurt all day," he said. "You know that, right?"

"That's what I *like* to eat," she replied, walking over to her dresser. She sat down, removed her ear studs, and placed them carefully in her jewelry box.

"But it's not healthy."

Vienna didn't respond. She *knew* that. But it was the only thing she could consistently eat. Sometimes she didn't even like that—and went a whole day without eating anything. She didn't know why. But she figured eating *something* was better than nothing.

Eden sighed. "I'm ordering for both of us," he said, leaving the room.

She stared at herself in the mirror. She looked healthy. Her cheeks weren't hollow, and her skin wasn't pale. She even looked radiant.

But what she did notice was that the guy who could tell she wasn't eating well... had somehow never noticed how his friends treated her.

Present

Vienna was left alone to pick up the bridesmaid dress by herself since Carmy was tired and wanted to sleep in. She couldn't fight that back, so she decided she'd pick it up herself — or else Petal was going to go crazy.

Romy and Petal had been so busy, she had barely seen them in the last couple of days. She'd been trying to help them out as much as possible, even though the people who usually handled those things had already arrived. One of the last things left to do was pick up the dress.

She entered the store and pulled out the bill from her tote bag, handing it to the person at the front desk. Amelie, whom she recognized from earlier, walked by. Amelie waved.

Vienna waved back. "Hi, how are you?"

"Great! The dress turned out amazing," she said. "By the way."

"I'm glad. It's my friend's big day," she said. "She wants everything to be perfect."

"It is perfect," Amelie said. "You have nothing to worry about."

The girl at the front desk brought out two black-covered hangers from the back. "One with a sweetheart neck and another with halter, both in emerald green?"

Vienna nodded. "Yes, that's right."

"I think the green is going to go so well with your red hair," Amelie said. "Have a great day. I'll get back to my work." She walked into the back of the store.

Vienna grabbed the clothes by the hangers. They seemed heavier than expected. "Thank you," she muttered, and left the store.

She mentally checked off one more thing from Petal's list. She walked down the street, making sure to lift the dresses as far from the ground as possible.

She noticed that the streets were pretty empty for a weekend — probably because the vacation season was over. The air was chillier, like it usually was during summer nights. She didn't know if the seasons had changed.

"Vivi?" she heard someone call out from across the street. She stopped short and looked at the opposite lane.

Eden stood there, in his brown jacket and black denim. His blonde hair went astray in the chill breeze. He waited for the vehicles to pass and crossed the road to reach her.

"We've got to stop running into each other like this."

Vienna nodded. "I agree." She had come to terms with the fact that the island was small, and she was going to run into people she didn't want to every time she stepped out. At that moment, she realized how lucky she was to live in a huge city where no one cares what or who anyone is.

"I'm just going to pick up something from the store for Nalia," he said.

She brought up the hangers and gave them a shake. "Picked up the bridesmaids' clothes," she said.

"That's nice," he said. "Big day is soon, huh?"

"In three days."

"About weddings," he started, "did you receive my wedding invitation?"

Vienna nodded. She didn't really want to get into it. "I did."

"I'm sorry if that was too much," he said. "Nalia heard from a friend about the hotel you guys were staying at, so she thought it'd be a good idea to send it."

"I understand," she said — even though she really didn't.

"I couldn't really stop her, cause..." He stopped, looked down at the ground, and then looked back up. "She doesn't really know about us."

"I got that from the conversation the other day."

He nodded again and pointed at the dress. "I can drop you," he said.

"No, it's fine," she said, looking away. The leaves on the tree above them were both green and yellow. She couldn't point out what kind of tree it was, though. "It's nearby."

"Vivi, just for old times' sake," he said. "Please?"

"I thought you said you had something to do?"

"I can just do it after I drop you off. You said it's not that far."

It seemed like he wouldn't let her go unless she agreed, so she did. She walked behind him to his parking spot.

"You got a rental on an island that's walkable?" she asked as she got into his grey Chevrolet Malibu.

He put his seat belt on. "Yeah, there's too much to buy and do just by walking."

Vienna nodded. The cold air from the AC blasted right into her face. The ride was quiet. She didn't really have anything to say, but she knew he had a lot to say — and he didn't say anything either.

"Congratulations on the wedding," she said. "If I hadn't already said."

"Thank you."

"I'm so happy for you," she said — and she meant it. "I'm just surprised to run into you getting married after all this time."

Eden laughed. "Life works in mysterious ways."

Vienna nodded. "Right."

By then, they had already reached Vienna's hotel. She didn't get out right away. Something was stopping her. She wished she could say something — anything — but there was nothing, really.

Just as she reached for the handle to exit, he held her arm to stop her, then quickly let go.

She looked at him, confused.

"I wish I did things differently back then," he said. "I regret a lot of things."

"You don't really have to say—" she started, but he cut her off.

"Let me finish," he said, and continued. "I don't regret that I met Nalia because of you, because I love her. But I never got over the way things ended between us. And for that, I'm always going to be sorry. I know it's too late, but I had to tell you this."

"That was three years ago," she said, sighing. "I didn't know what was going on with me. I still don't. You don't have anything to regret. And you don't have to be sorry."

Eden nodded. "But do you ever regret?"

Vienna looked up at the roof of the car. The black fuzzy lining bounced the sunlight that passed through the window. She breathed in audibly.

"No," she muttered.

Eden looked straight ahead. "Well, good luck with your life," he said, not looking at her.

"You too," Vienna said, grabbing the door handle.

She was instantly hit by the bright sunlight as he drove off — and that was the last time she ever saw Eden, whether on the island or back in her city.

CHAPTER XXVIII

Past

Vienna was back at *Decords*, but this time with Eden, who said he'd tag along. Honestly, she just wanted peace of mind, and as usual, she naturally wanted to come to *Decords* — but Eden mentioned he had a couple of things to pick up, so there they were, looking at overpriced coasters.

"I have a couple of books at your place, by the way," she said, picking up a blue coaster with fishes painted on it. "I'll come by later and get them?"

Eden nodded. He was holding a basket filled with a bunch of towels and porcelain toothbrush holders. She didn't understand why something that's going to be in the bathroom had to be porcelain, but she left Eden to his liking.

She put the coaster down. "I can find you much better ones at, like, the dollar store or something," she said, picking up another one — black with gold paint splattered over it. "This is just ridiculous for something so insignificant."

"I know," he said, looking at the coaster she was holding. "But my mom always tells me to get my home goods from here." He picked up the coaster's pair. "I like this."

Vienna didn't, but she wasn't going to say that. He'd already set his mind to get it, so she just nodded. "Good choice."

She went to the bedroom section while Eden looked at coffee mugs. The beds were set up in a way that made them look like the bedroom of someone you'd know. It was always comforting to her — finding that she could get a sense of home away from home at a home décor store.

She lay on the bed with blue covers and mirrors patterned in a way that formed a flower. The roof was pale blue — two shades lighter than the covers on the bed. A chandelier in the middle of the ceiling seemed too huge. It wasn't lit, so she wondered if it had white or gold lighting, but she knew she'd never come to know it.

It suddenly struck her that she never really fit in at *Decords*. It was simply a shelter — a place that made her feel good for a while whenever she felt down. There were a lot of things she'd never come to know — like the light of the chandelier, or what people did with patterned mirrors on their bed's headrest, or why people used coasters like Eden did.

She got up and walked to where Eden was. He was now looking at soap trays. She recognized one from a year ago, when she had met Eden right at this store — the clam-shaped soap tray.

But he picked up the one shaped like a seashell. There wasn't much of a difference between the clam and the seashell — they were just shaped differently, though the texture was the same. They came in three different colors with a shiny tint.

"Should I get the black or green?" he said, holding one in each hand.

As she saw him debating what to get, she realized that this wasn't where she belonged. Not between expensive soap trays and coasters — or with Eden, who seemed to effortlessly know what he wanted and stood right where he belonged.

"I want to break up," she said.

She hadn't meant for that to slip out, but deep down, she knew exactly what she meant.

Eden looked at her, putting down the soap trays. "What?"

"You heard me," she said.

"No, I don't think I heard you well," he said, placing the basket on the ground.

"We're just too different, Eden," she said, shaking her head in dismay.

"So what?" he said, running his fingers through his hair. He looked visibly shaken. "I like that about us."

"Well, I don't," she said. "I'm going to walk away from this place, and I don't want you to follow me."

"Vienna," he said, his voice pleading. "Why are you doing this?"

"I don't know," she said, her eyes brimming with tears — she started walking toward the entrance and never stopped until she reached home.

He didn't follow her, just like she'd asked.

Several months followed where she ignored his calls — even the time he showed up at her door once, and she refused to open it. She withdrew from society, except when Petal and Carmy came by to visit once in a while.

And then the calls stopped. Eden was completely out of her life.

Vienna was slowly integrating herself back into society, but just without Eden. She thought the deep sadness she felt within would be gone from her system like Eden was — but the sadness stayed.

She did think about him a lot. She wished she'd given him the explanation she very much owed him, at the very least. But more than anything, she wished that the last time she saw him hadn't been at *Decords* — and that she'd run into him at least once again.

That happened three years later, halfway across the world. She was still at a loss for words, but Eden seemed to have forgotten and forgiven.

Yet Vienna stood with the same feelings she'd had the last time she saw him: sadness, and hatred for self.

CHAPTER XXIX

Present

It was the day of Petal's wedding. Everyone seemed to be in a hurry—but the good kind. So much laughter and so many unfamiliar faces. Vienna adjusted her hair that was blowing into her mouth.

Carmy waved to her boyfriend, who was sitting at the back. Vienna smiled at her when she looked back.

"I can't believe Marcus came all the way here," Carmy said. "I am so happy."

Vienna could tell. Everyone seemed happy. It was the kind of day that made it feel like even if something went wrong, it would still be okay. She almost smiled at the thought—because if she said that out loud in front of Petal, she'd be so disappointed in her need for perfection.

The wedding venue was breathtaking—a soft stretch of golden sand, waves rolling gently onto the shore, and an aisle lined with delicate white petals that contrasted beautifully against the deep blue of the ocean. The sun was beginning to dip lower in the sky, casting everything in a warm, golden glow.

A wooden arch stood at the end of the aisle, wrapped in twisting vines of white roses and baby's breath. Beneath it, a white linen canopy fluttered in the salty breeze, framing the place where Petal and Romy would soon stand.

Vienna took a deep breath, letting the scent of the sea and fresh flowers settle into her senses.

She wasn't usually someone who got swept up in moments like this, but today felt different. Special.

Then, the music started. It was a piece Vienna couldn't recognize, but it was a very melodious quartet piece.

Everyone turned.

Romy was the first to walk down the aisle, arm in arm with her father.

Her dress was ethereal—soft, flowing fabric that moved like water with every step. The bodice was adorned with tiny pearls and floral embroidery—subtle but stunning—and the sleeves draped off her shoulders in delicate, airy folds. She looked completely in her element—barefoot, smiling, radiating happiness.

Vienna couldn't help but watch Petal's reaction instead.

Petal was standing at the entrance now, and for the first time in forever, she looked completely still.

Not worried. Not controlling.

Just soft. Just in love.

And then she walked forward.

Her dress was different from Romy's—structured, elegant, with a fitted bodice and delicate lace trailing down the long, flowing skirt. A veil that started plain from the head but slowly trailed down with embroidery of petals falling—fitting her name.

The lace caught the sunlight, creating a faint shimmer with every step. Her hair was pinned back with tiny white blossoms, and as she walked, she barely looked at anyone else.

Only at Romy.

Vienna felt something tighten in her chest.

The ceremony itself was simple—vows spoken softly over the sound of the waves, laughter when Romy almost tripped in the sand, and an overwhelming warmth in the air as they exchanged rings.

Then, finally, the "You may kiss."

Vienna didn't realize she was smiling until it happened.

Romy pulled Petal in immediately, hands on her waist, lips pressed together in a kiss that was met with cheers, applause, and the crashing of waves behind them.

Carmy clapped beside her, wiping away tears. Vienna nudged and hugged Carmy slightly.

"They did it," Carmy whispered, smiling widely, though the tears were still falling.

Vienna exhaled, nodding.

"They did."

And for the first time that day, she felt completely, undeniably present.

• • •

It was the wedding evening. Everyone was gathered, music blasting loudly. Vienna ate a couple of things and called it a day since she was full. She stuck to eating the Champagne Dreams with Lemon Chiffon cake, which seemed to be a hit among the crowd.

Carmy and Marcus were talking beside her; Petal and Romy were laughing a few seats away at something someone said. Everyone was in their own world, and she was lost in thought, wondering if she was going to mess up her speech.

"I think you should do the toast now," Carmy said, lightly touching Vienna's shoulder. She smiled and got up, picking up a fork next to her plate of cake on the table. She tapped it against the wine glass filled with water. The room fell silent. Everyone looked at her with their full attention.

"Oh wow, hello everyone," she said, laughing awkwardly and adjusting the sweetheart neckline of her dress, pulling it up. "I'm not really a people person, but I'd do anything my best friend Petal asks me to—so bear with me."

This pulled out a few laughs from the crowd.

She took a breath in and looked at Romy and Petal, who were hand in hand and seemed so in love. She smiled.

"We've known each other for a decade now. We've seen all sides of each other. Whatever emotions we felt, they were shared between the three of us. But then Petal fell in love—a side we'd never witnessed hit upon us. She was so in love. We'd never seen her like that before. And knowing Petal, she has so much love to give—and that just doubled in size with Romy, who is simply a bundle of joy."

She took a moment to look at Carmy, who nodded, her eyes glistening.

"A couple of days ago, at the bachelorette party, we talked about a game we made up. It's stupid, really," she laughed, so did Petal, who was shaking her head and waving her hand. "It was this game where we brought out a deck of cards and a pair of dice. We had to decide on number 216—which was your 'to-be'—and pull-out number cards from the deck, hoping the sum matched your chosen number. If it didn't, you got to roll the dice—which we called the 'maybe'—hoping the sum of those numbers would help match your to-be."

Vienna laughed, reminiscing. "It was a dumb game. Too many numbers for me to work with, really. Our numbers almost never matched. But what we did talk about the other day was that despite the 'to-bes' and 'maybes,' the constants were just us hoping, staying, waiting for the numbers to show up. Those constants in my life also happened to be my best friends. And now one of them is in your life, Romy." Vienna felt a pang of sadness while she saw Petal look at Romy with nothing but love.

She turned slightly to face the rest of the crowd and back to her friends. "I hope you guys have a long game of to-bes and maybes. Even though it was a dumb game, we chose to play it—much like life. But the people playing along with you are the best part of it."

CHAPTER XXX

Present

It was the day when they had to leave the island—to go back to the city, back to normal, boring life—so Vienna decided to take a detour around the island, walking. She was hoping she didn't run into anyone anymore; she was tired of it. She wanted to have one day to herself and her thoughts alone.

In a place where the sounds of waves seemed to drown out all other noise, they couldn't seem to drown out her thoughts much like on her first day at the island. But she didn't know what she was thinking about either—a bunch of stuff that didn't make sense to her, even to her.

She sometimes felt like she was dissociating. As she walked mindlessly into a dimly lit street with barely any people on it, she noticed a bookstore. Almost like it was nestled away from the noisy tourists. The irony of it hit her heavily too. She walked in and was instantly taken in by the fragrance of rosewood and sandalwood. She smiled—she knew the familiarity of bookstores that smelled like forests and lakes, a comfort she was happy to find away from her room's bookshelves.

Vienna traced the carved wood frame of the bookshelf; floral vines spread across it. As she looked up, there was a white rectangular panel with big black, bold letters referring to the genres.

She went by the non-fiction section. So many self-help books lined the racks. She wondered if everyone else was just as lost as her—to pick up one of these books and learn from it, knowing that maybe if someone can't understand them, they'll alter themselves into someone who can be understood.

She just looked around, not really touching anything. She wished she'd spent more time looking around the island while she was there—she could've found the bookstore earlier. She liked the comfort she found in bookstores. They just made her feel more alive. She didn't know why, because she hated reading as a child, but one day she decided to get into it and then never stopped.

Vienna looked around to see if there was a shopkeeper, but there was no one to be found. It was like the place had just spawned out of nowhere—but she heard rustling from upstairs and knew someone was there, keeping the place alive.

A bitter taste settled in her mouth when she thought about having to leave. She wasn't one to get attached to anyone or anything, but something about this place just told her she'd think about it for a long time. A time that felt like something straight from one of the books on the shelf.

She walked further into the store, her hands absent-mindedly trailing along the spines of the books. Some were old and worn—showing clear signs of being previously loved and adored—while some were brand new. A small woven rug lay in the center of the floor, slightly worn at the edges, and in the corner, a tiny seating area with a mismatched armchair and a stack of books on a side table.

She liked, or maybe even loved, this place. Not just the bookstore, but the island in general. The way she could see the sea from her room and fall asleep to the sound of waves. Even though she missed her cat, Lucky, from back home, she realized that the thought of going back to sleep to the sounds of a city that never slept didn't excite her anymore—it only made her ache.

She pulled out a book at random and flipped it open. Her eyes weren't really following the words because her mind was elsewhere—about leaving, going back to the city, working. Now that everyone had settled into their own lives, she was left alone to finally figure out what she wanted to do with hers. It wasn't like she wasn't content with what she had—but she had to figure out where to put this sadness that had been weighing down on her for ages, the kind she'd refused to acknowledge.

She closed the book and put it back into its place, then walked up the stairs leading to more sections of books. That area seemed to be designed for children with a huge window facing straight at the sea, with a children's book section and an astronomy shelf right beside it.

There were colorful little wooden chairs, and Vienna almost smiled to herself looking at them. A bunch of toys were scattered around, and a scooter sat a little away from the chairs. She looked up—the roof was painted blue with white clouds, and golden lights hung from above. She suddenly felt a warmth within herself.

Vienna took a slow step forward, her fingers grazing the edge of one of the tiny wooden chairs. The paint was slightly chipped at the corners, revealing the natural wood underneath. It looked lived-in, like a place that had been loved.

The toys scattered around the floor—a stuffed rabbit missing an ear, a plastic dinosaur, a few crayons rolling near the base of a bookshelf—made the space feel less like a store and more like someone's quiet little world.

Something about it made her chest ache, but in a way she couldn't quite place.

It was the kind of place she wished she had found when she was younger. A place where time slowed, where things felt softer, safer.

She walked toward the astronomy section. She didn't really pay attention to the titles, but one caught her eye on the very last row. It seemed familiar. She sat down to pull it, and her chest instantly tightened at the title.

A Guide to the Moon and Stars.

Vienna walked back to where the tiny chairs facing the window were and sat down on one of them—even though she didn't really fit. It felt comfortable to make herself as small as possible at that moment. She had the same book back home. She remembered the day she got it like it was yesterday—at a thrift store. The one she held now was new and untouched, while the one Carmy got her about four years ago was already worn out, with multiple notes written in it.

She never read the book after taking it home—just the one note that was sprawled across one of the pages. But she remembered the day. How much she missed just doing life—as simple as walking into a thrift store with her best friends to spontaneously buy a book she'd never read again but would hold so much emotional weight for her even after years.

In the middle of the children's reading room whilst staring at the soundless view of the sea, she finally broke down.